PARROT WOMAN

OTHER YEARLING BOOKS YOU WILL ENJOY:

PARROT WOMAN

by Alice Bach

A YEARLING BOOK

Published by
Dell Publishing Co., Inc.
1 Dag Hammarskjold Plaza
New York, New York 10017

Yearling ® TM 913705, Dell Publishing Co., Inc.

ISBN: 0-440-46987-2

Printed in the United States of America

December 1987

10 9 8 7 6 5 4 3 2 1

CW

For Cheryl Exum,
who lives by this business of words.

"Forsan et haec olim meminisse iuvabit."
                                        —Virgil

Chapter One

I'd been standing around on the downtown subway platform for almost half an hour waiting for a train. This wait did not sweeten my disposition, as my mother would say. I'd promised my best friend, Stanwyck Baum, that I'd pick her up to go shopping by ten thirty, but it was ten thirty before the train even pulled into the station. There was a going-out-of-business sale at some hot boutique in the East Village, and Stanwyck was desperate to get there before the sweaters had been picked over. This was Stanwyck's year for sweaters.

It was the first truly warm Saturday of the year, one week into our winter recess—my favorite school holiday. If nature cooperates, you leave school in your winter coat and return after the holiday in a light jacket. This year we had to endure one of those nasty winters, with March roaring in like a lion, the favorite expression of TV weather wimps. Blustery winds had slapped my face every gray morning on the way to school, and sleeting snow had fallen from very gray skies all during March. Today the warm sun had encouraged half of New York to go shopping as a reward for getting through another winter.

The train that finally came was crowded, mostly with women holding the hands of restless children, for whom shopping was clearly no treat. I glanced at the row of ads above the windows of the train. Among the laxatives and aspirin and remedies for aching joints, there was a picture of Stanwyck's father. Mel Baum, the Mattress King, famous all over the city, was sprawled on a humongous king-size mattress, his hands outstretched. "Sleep with me tonight," his ads read. "Tomorrow morning you'll wake up a new person."

The joke is that Mel Baum is as unlikely a sex symbol as you could imagine. In the ads, even dressed in a tuxedo, he looks like a large stuffed toy grinning at the camera. His long face and sad, pouchy eyes are like a basset hound's. Bald and not exactly in peak condition, Mel Baum parodies a sexy man as he pleads with New York to try a night on a Baum mattress. His ad agency insists that the sexy tone of the ads is responsible for Mel being number one in New York. Maybe so, but ever since the campaign began last fall, Stanwyck has had to take a lot of teasing about her father propositioning New York in subway ads and in his famous late-night TV spot: "If you were watching this show on a Baum mattress, you'd be asleep by now."

The train pulled into the Spring Street station. I ran up the stairs and hurried down Spring Street. It was a surprise to feel the warm sun on my face. I straightened up, realizing I had wrapped my scarf across my face, as if the winter wind would be attacking me. Talk about habit! It was after eleven. I was almost an hour late. I half expected to see Stanwyck standing outside the subway station, her dark face squinting into the sunlight, irritated because I'd kept her waiting. I turned the corner onto Prince and unbuttoned my coat. It might even be warm enough today to have lunch in the park.

As I approached the middle of the block where the Baums' loft is, I saw several TV cameras and a knot of people standing in the narrow street. They seemed to be waiting for someone to come out of the building. Suddenly a couple of gray cars pulled up, and the people hurried to the curb. Two men jumped out of the first car, and one talked into a walkie-talkie. He turned and saluted a man standing in a doorway across the street from where I was standing. The cameramen jockeyed for position. They must be making a movie, I thought. Two more men got out of the second car, and one pulled out a piece of paper from the breast pocket of his jacket. The reporters with microphones made a half-circle around him. I moved closer to hear what they were saying.

"We are here this morning to announce a major arrest that will end a ring of international smugglers of rare birds into this city. The FBI, working with the Border Patrol and the undercover investigation unit of the City of New York, has spent months tracking down the international ring of smugglers. A worldwide operation, we have proof that the group operates out of Rio de Janeiro and Bahia in Brazil. With the cooperation of Interpol, we are preparing to make arrests in Venezuela and Argentina before the end of the week."

"What is the New York connection?" asked one of the reporters. I looked closely and realized she was Eileen McKinnon of the Channel 6 evening news team. This wasn't a make-believe police bust. It was the real thing. I wondered why Stanwyck hadn't seen all the commotion outside her building and come down to investigate. Usually TV cameras attract Stanwyck like magnets. As I moved toward the front door of the building, one of the men barred my entrance.

"Sorry, miss, but this building is sealed for the time being. Official police business."

"But my friend lives here, on the third floor. I'm supposed to meet her. We're going shopping."

"Sorry, you'll have to wait. I have my orders. No one goes in or out. All the tenants have been notified—"

"You mean the people who live here know what's going on out here?"

"Sure do." He grinned. "You lucked out. You'll get to see a real FBI arrest. Maybe get on TV yourself." He smiled as if I were six years old.

"I've been on TV many times," I said, feeling foolish as soon as the words were out of my mouth. It was certainly strange that, if Stanwyck knew about the FBI making an arrest, she wasn't in the thick of it.

"Could you tell us why these birds are valuable? I mean, what's the big deal with a few parrots?" A reporter pulled out a notebook, and a cameraman filmed him intensely scribbling notes, although the FBI man hadn't yet begun to answer the question.

A second reporter pushed his microphone closer to the FBI guy. "I didn't know you guys were in the business of protecting birds. I mean, there must be uglier crimes than black-market birds going on in this city."

The FBI man snickered at the reporter. "The black market in these birds would surprise you. Two blocks from here, an African Gray Parrot with scarlet-tinged wings was sold to one of our undercover guys last week for eighteen hundred dollars. And that's a relatively common bird. They fill orders like that every day." He glanced at his typed sheet. "We have information that a Red-Bellied Conure from the southeastern part of Brazil was sold last month for five thousand." He looked directly into the camera lens. "The bird has been traced to this neighborhood."

Eileen McKinnon stepped out in front of the other reporters. "Will you be arresting the owner? Can we get a shot of this Red-Bellied whatever?"

He shook his head. "The trail on the bird has gone cold. The man we are arresting is not a receiver of the birds. He's the New York connection to the entire ring." He shuffled his papers for effect. "We have telephone bills for the last month to his South American contacts totaling nearly six thousand dollars. They clearly establish the connection between this man's business and outposts in Bahia, Rio de Janeiro, and the Paris Peninsula on the Venezuelan mainland." He squared his shoulders. The other FBI guys moved toward the front door of the building, as if on a prearranged signal. "We never arrest anyone until we're sure."

Suddenly, the door opened and two men stepped out, holding a third man by his arms. I gasped. The FBI men were holding Mel Baum as if he were their criminal.

I grabbed Eileen McKinnon's arm. "They've made a mistake! That's Mr. Baum—he's my friend Stanwyck's father. He's no smuggler. He owns a factory where they make mattresses."

Annoyed at this outburst, the FBI man shook his head.

11

"Get that kid out of here," he snapped to the man next to him, who pushed me out of the range of the cameras. "Over here, miss," he said, giving me no choice.

Having regained his composure, the FBI guy was talking into Eileen McKinnon's microphone. "Naturally, we are completely familiar with this man's background. His office and staff have been under surveillance for more than a month. It is clear that the Baum mattress company is a front for the largest smuggling operation of rare birds in the history of this country." He finished with a flourish and smiled an oily grin into the camera.

Then Stanwyck charged through the door with her mother close behind her. "You're all crazy! My father isn't guilty of anything!"

Two agents hustled Mel Baum into the backseat of the second gray car. Another agent jumped into the front seat. Poor Mr. Baum kept his head down and hadn't said a word. I ran to Stanwyck and tried to restrain her. But she broke away from me and socked the FBI agent on the shoulder. "My father wouldn't know a cockatoo from a canary! We've never owned even a dime-store parakeet. He doesn't even feed pigeons in the park!" She burst into tears.

"Although we hate to make an arrest publicly," an agent explained, "and we certainly didn't intend to embarrass this girl and her family, we decided to act openly at the request of the Brazilian and Venezuelan governments. These birds are endangered species, and it is illegal to export them for any reason. Their exquisite plumage brings a large price. If governments don't protect them from local poachers and

12

international organized crime, the birds will disappear from the earth."

One of the other agents began passing out press releases to the journalists. "It's important to emphasize that, dead or alive, the birds' worst enemy is man."

As if on cue, a middle-aged man with long gray hair in a sweatshirt that read OUR PLANET IS AN ENDANGERED SPECIES on the front stepped out of a car across the street. His arms were wrapped around a black plastic trash bag. He nodded to the agents and to the members of the press.

"I'm Jeremiah Roberts from the Society of Aviculturists. We have been working closely with the U.S. government and with representatives of the Brazilian government to prevent the slaughter of these precious birds." He cleared his throat and peered into the nearest camera lens as if there were an exotic bird trapped inside it.

"These beauties should be exported only to competent aviculturists who are committed to the breeding and preservation of each species. Thirty-nine species of rare birds have become extinct in the past twenty years because of the ignorance and greed of human beings. If vicious, unprincipled smugglers aren't stopped, these exotic, darling creatures may never again be seen on the face of the earth." He overturned his trash bag, and a mound of brightly colored feathers fell to the ground.

At the sight of the feathers, his mood turned angry. "Carnage! Carnage!" he shouted into the camera. His long fingers picked among the feathers. Then he held up a brilliant golden-yellow feather with pinkish-orange tips. "This is a flight feather from a Janday Conure. Probably the most lovely of all semi-tamed conures. Flight feathers! This is definitive evidence of foul play. Conures don't molt flight feathers."

"What film! This is going to be the story of the day." One of the reporters chuckled. "I thought it was going to be a routine bust. Jerry, get a close-up of that guy. He doesn't look like he's wrapped too tight. One of those nutcakes, no doubt. And zero in on the piles of feathers. Let's take a handful back to the studio in case they want to do some in-studio business." He leaned over and stuffed his pocket with feathers.

One of the other reporters tapped Roberts on the shoulder. "We'd like to get an interview with you, up close and personal."

"Be careful!" Roberts snapped at him. "These feathers are the only remains of the victims. They should be treated with respect."

"What did he say the name of his group was? Never heard of it," one of the journalists asked another.

"These ecology groups spring up like mushrooms after rain," answered his friend.

The agent in charge seemed anxious to regain control of the news conference. "These feathers and another bag that we've impounded for evidence were all found in the garbage Dumpster outside this very building, the residence of Mr. Mel Baum."

At the sound of her father's name, Stanwyck became alert again. "Anyone in the world could have left those feathers there. If he were guilty, why would he dump the evidence outside our house?"

"People get too sure of themselves, think they're above

the law. That's when we catch them." The FBI man smiled, folded the paper, put it back into his pocket, and addressed the reporters. "We'll have the arraignment downtown early this afternoon so you'll have plenty of time to process the film before you go on the air at six."

As he spoke, a slight wind blew from the west and stirred up the mound of feathers at his feet. Several stuck to the FBI agent's coat. He leaned over and plucked them off, but as soon as he got rid of one handful, a fresh wad blew onto his coat. Stanwyck leaned over and dumped a handful onto his hair. Two of the reporters burst out laughing.

Clearly furious, the agent hurried back to his car, still trying to brush the evidence from his coat. The reporters made sure their cameras had captured the agent desperately swiping at the feathers in his hair.

The gray cars sped off, and the reporters waited at the curb, talking quietly while the cameramen packed the equipment into the TV vans. I hurried over to Stanwyck, who was clutching her mother. Both of them were pale and seemed only partially aware of all the activity around them.

"Jess"—Mrs. Baum made an effort to smile—"I'm sorry you had to witness this terrible business."

Stanwyck shook her head angrily. "Nonsense! Daddy didn't do anything. This is a frame-up. They can't arrest citizens as if they were criminals."

"They just did," I said, regretting the words as soon as they were out of my mouth.

They had a chilling effect on Stanwyck. Her anger drained out of her, and she started to tremble. "Mommy, what are we going to do? What if they never believe Daddy? What if they send him to jail?"

"Let's go back upstairs, girls." Mrs. Baum seemed to gather strength from Stanwyck's desperate tears. "We have to wait for David Sheldon to get here. As soon as they've arranged for bail for your father downtown, he'll come over and explain everything to us." She put her arms around Stan's sagging shoulders. "Let's get away from this unpleasant scene and these awful feathers."

I glanced over my shoulder. Feathers were clinging to the lower branches of the plane tree and to the bushes planted underneath the tree. The brightly colored feathers gave the street an oddly festive air, as if some partygoers had just passed by.

As we went through the lobby, the people who live in the other lofts stopped talking. They had watched the whole scene through the one-way picture window in the lobby. The Japanese architect who lives on the top floor handed Mrs. Baum the key to the elevator. "You have competent legal advice? Mel has the best lawyers?"

"I don't know if they're the best lawyers, Mifune, but they promised me that Mel would be back home before dinnertime."

"What does the FBI say he did?"

"Something about smuggling exotic birds." Mrs. Baum shrugged. "I don't have a clear picture of the charges, but I know he never made those phone calls to Brazil—although they showed us the records, page after page of them. It was his private phone line at the factory. No mistake about that. I saw it myself."

Mifune laughed. "Maybe it is Stanwyck and her friends on the computer?"

16

"Trapping my own father?" Stanwyck pushed her mother into the elevator.

"Now, dear, you're going to have to watch your temper. We can't help your father unless we remain totally in control of our emotions. Try to remember that people mean well. Everyone loves your father. All the factory people will be calling, and we must treat them kindly."

"Did you hear what that turkey said?" Stanwyck whined.

"FBI agents swarming over the building is just as puzzling to Mifune as it is to us. And it's not as if you and your friends have an unblemished record. You almost went to jail yourselves for getting involved in those computer bulletin board games."

Mrs. Baum was referring to a scheme of Freddy Frobisher's in which Stanwyck had unwittingly participated with other phreakers through her bulletin board last year, to crack computer games. But Stanwyck had sworn off breaking into computer databanks. She appeared to have lost interest in playing tricks with the computer and used it only in the normal school ways. She'd given her BBS files and the much-desired title *sysop*—the person who directs a bulletin board—to our friend Noah. She'd retired from the business. She hadn't spoken to Freddy since she'd found out he was the swine who had sabotaged her BBS.

"Mom, you know none of my friends would frame Daddy, don't you?" Stanwyck filled the kettle with water and put it on the stove. I got out the teacups and a few boxes of herb tea. Stan and her mother are both herb-tea addicts.

Mrs. Baum absently licked a spoonful of honey. "I suppose so. But how do we explain your father being charged with all those calls?"

17

"I don't know, but Jess and I are going to find out." She glared at me as if I'd been idly dialing Rio in my spare time.

"Don't look so angry, Stan. I'm totally innocent. I'm not even sure where Venezuela is," I said, reaching for a ginger cookie. It was slowly sinking in that the FBI had actually arrested Mr. Baum in front of TV cameras. "Do you know, or do they know, *why* your father was smuggling those birds? I mean, *supposedly* smuggling those birds."

They both shook their heads. The telephone rang. Mrs. Baum pulled the phone toward her and picked up the receiver. "Hello? Who? No, we have no comment. My husband is absolutely innocent." She hung up and sighed. "I guess we can expect a lot of calls. That was one of the wire services. They'll spread this story all over the country." She looked over to the window. "I guess nobody's totally innocent."

"Daddy is," insisted Stanwyck.

"I suppose he's claimed lowest sale prices when they haven't actually been the lowest sale prices."

"Mom, this is no time to become a consumer advocate."

Mrs. Baum nodded. "I hope your poor father isn't having too hard a time with those FBI people."

"Daddy can take care of himself," Stanwyck said bravely, but her voice was as hollow as her mother's.

Chapter Two

It was almost three o'clock before David Sheldon, Mr.
Baum's attorney, arrived at the loft. There had been count-
less phone calls. A few were from people who worked at the
factory wanting to know how they could help. One was from
the phone company, saying there had been a report of
trouble on the line. That made me laugh till my sides ached.
There had been calls from newspapers as far away as Chicago
and St. Louis. One woman called and started screaming that
Mel Baum was murdering birds and she hoped he got the
electric chair. After that, you could hardly blame us for
taking the phone off the hook.

Mrs. Baum was pacing around the loft. Stanwyck was
lying on the couch with a pillow over half her face as if she
had an earache. From time to time I went to the window to
look down onto the street. Across the street a woman in a
dark coat was leaning against the front of the building scanning the sky. She was very pale and thin, with dank black
hair. I thought she looked like a crow. Then I laughed at
myself for thinking bird thoughts.

There was no one else on the street. Most of the feathers had finally blown away; I was glad those last vestiges of the morning's bizarre scene were gone. Now, if only Mr. Baum would walk through the door and assure us all that it had been a silly mistake!

As if reading my mind, Stanwyck tossed her pillow onto the floor. "I hope Daddy sues the hell out of the FBI for false arrest. I bet this whole thing will be over in a couple of hours and we can all go out for a big dinner. I hope that stinker in the gray car has to go on TV and apologize to Daddy formally."

"And that they all lose their jobs," I added eagerly, "and their gray cars."

"People never remember apologies. I doubt the TV stations would send out camera crews for something as unexciting as your father coming home not guilty," Mrs. Baum said bitterly. "It's only the scandals they flock to."

The doorbell rang. We all looked at each other. Finally, Mrs. Baum walked toward the door. "Got to remain calm for your father's sake," she said, pausing in front of the mirror for a moment to smooth her hair.

"Hello, David. Thank goodness you've come. Where's Mel?" Mrs. Baum's voice rose in alarm. "They are going to let him out?"

"Now, don't get all worked up, Loretta. We've got a long way to go. They've set bail, and as soon as Mel's banker gets the paperwork down to the court, he'll be free to come home."

"You didn't leave Daddy alone?" Stanwyck leaped off the couch and ran over to Mr. Sheldon and her mother.

20

"Two of my partners are there, Stanwyck. And half our research staff. He's got more lawyers than the feds have." He laughed and tossed his coat onto the chair. "I've assigned three of our best young lawyers to work here as soon as Mel gets out. We need to look through the receipts for the past five years to prove that Mel's record is as clean as a whistle."

"Is it clean?" Mrs. Baum asked, twisting her hands in her lap. "I mean, it's hard to believe the federal government could make a mistake."

"My dear Loretta, if they didn't make mistakes, I'd be out of work." Mr. Sheldon smiled at all of us, telegraphing confidence. I felt like a member of a jury. He looked at Stanwyck. "I could use some coffee. We got the judge to agree to sign a gag order on the government for the next forty-eight hours. So there won't be too many press reports issued after tonight's circus on the news. You'd all better prepare yourselves. That's going to be a disaster." He looked at me questioningly.

"I'm Jess Graham," I said quickly, "Stanwyck's friend."

"Oh yes, now I recall. You were implicated with Stanwyck in that computer-fraud business. Now, you girls don't know anything about those calls to South America, do you? If you do, now is the time—"

"How could you think we'd frame Daddy?" Stanwyck slammed a coffee mug onto the counter.

"No one's saying you did it intentionally. Maybe you thought it would be a challenge—you know, like the last time? Maybe you wanted to see if you could dial up Brazil and nobody would find out."

"Stop talking as if I were a child," snapped Stanwyck. "I

21

never dialed Brazil in my life. It's inconceivable to me that dialing a phone could be a challenge."

Even I looked skeptical at Stanwyck's heated denial.

Mrs. Baum shook Stanwyck gently by the shoulder. "Don't be rude, Stanwyck. You *are* the likeliest suspect. You have to admit that your past record of computer phreaking is incriminating. Come to think of it, I'm surprised they didn't arrest you instead of your poor father." Mrs. Baum sat down and stacked up several herb tea boxes.

"They're right, Stanwyck." I sat across the table from Mr. Sheldon. "What proof do we have that it isn't a phreak? Somebody might have been phreaking in your name. Another Freddy Frobisher."

"Do you have a copy of the phone charges?" Stan asked the lawyer. "We'll have to analyze them and see if a pattern emerges and then see if we can trace the phreak—if it is a phreak, which I doubt." Stanwyck pushed her hair behind her ears and sat down at the table. "It's better than sitting around feeling helpless." She took the sheaf of stapled pages that Mr. Sheldon handed her and motioned me to pull my chair alongside hers.

"It's obvious. The calls are made every ten minutes over a three-hour period for the first day. Jess, run down the first column on each page and see if the pattern continues that way. I'll check the list of destination numbers for a pattern."

We worked with pencil and paper in silence for about half an hour. Mrs. Baum and Mr. Sheldon talked quietly at the far end of the loft under the large windows. They had their backs to us, looking out at the street, as if the answer to this puzzle could be found at the spot where they had arrested Mel Baum.

I was surprised to see discernible patterns. Each call had lasted a minute or less. On no day had there been less than a linked group of ten calls. On six days there had been ten calls over a one-hour period. On most days there had been thirty calls in three hours.

Stan was having a more difficult time with the calls to Brazil and Venezuela. "They don't form a pattern," she reported, a look of dejection on her face. "Most of them are to Brazil, but the Venezuela entries are not at any particular intervals."

"What about the numbers?" I asked.

Mr. Sheldon glanced over my shoulder and read the notes on my pad. "We all noticed the pattern of the timed intervals, girls. I don't want to burst your bubble, but it is the government's contention that your father made those calls every ten minutes as a signal to his partners south of the border. They think the calls themselves were of no importance, but rather that the pattern of the calls, their frequency, is what is significant."

"What made them reach that conclusion?" asked Stanwyck, sucking on the end of her pencil.

"I pointed out that the calls didn't last longer than a few seconds. What kind of smuggling ring would that be?" He flung out his arms dramatically. Then he shrugged. "They weren't impressed by my reasoning. They put forth their theory, which they then insisted was proved by the enormous number of calls, which had to be a signal to someone!"

Stan stood up quickly, knocking over her chair. "I can't stand it anymore. Let's get out of here, Jess. Please?"

I stood up, seeing tears in my friend's eyes. "Of course. Where do you want to go?"

"I don't care. Let's walk around. Maybe the wind in my face will make me feel less hopeless." She pulled on her jacket and looked at her watch. "When do you think Daddy will be back?" she asked Mr. Sheldon in a small, childlike voice.

"Probably before suppertime," he said in a kindlier tone. "Don't be frightened, Stanwyck. Our firm has an excellent research staff. Each one is from a top law school. Although they're not used to dealing with major criminal matters, they'll pull out the facts and get this thing straightened out. You've got my word for it."

When we got into the lobby, Stanwyck grabbed my hand. "We can't depend on Sheldon's research staff. I've heard Dad say Sheldon couldn't get a suspended sentence for a dog who urinated on a police-station hydrant. We have to save my dad, Jess. Are you with me?"

"Of course," I answered solemnly.

We walked a block in silence. "Where do we start?" I asked timidly.

Stan didn't answer immediately. Pausing in front of a stationery store, she said, "You buy a couple of small notebooks and pens. I'll study the phone book near the booth in the back of the store. We've got to establish a working list of pet stores. Then we can start becoming parrot experts. So many pounds of feathers stuffed into garbage cans in the neighborhood clearly means there are lots of parrots living in some of these buildings. We've got to find out where."

"Find the parrots, and we find the real criminals," I said, filled with admiration.

There were seven pet stores below Thirty-fourth Street, most with cute names like Puppies 'n Things and The Cat's Meow. From the store names, there didn't seem to be any store devoted to parrots. There was no Parrots 'n Things a block from where we were standing to make our job easier.

"Let's take a cab to this Dogeteria place on Twenty-fifth. Their ad says everything for dogs, cats, fish, and birds." Stanwyck's cheeks had a light flush. She was coming back to life.

"It won't be a bird-specialty place," I objected.

"But if we are run-of-the-mill kids anxious to buy a parrot that talks, we'd go to a large pet store and hope for the best. And that's exactly what we're going to be—kids trying to buy a parrot."

We hailed a cab, and a few minutes later we were outside the Dogeteria. It looked like a supermarket, with doggie juice and doggie dishes and shelf after shelf of every imaginable variety of doggie stew. In the window of the store were stuffed dogs wearing coats with fur collars, rhinestone-studded leashes, and tiny pairs of red boots.

Stanwyck strode quickly to the back of the store, where a fat bald man dressed in a white doctor's coat was holding a small Dalmatian puppy. A woman in a fur coat and fur hat was shaking her head. "He doesn't do anything. He just lies in the corner with his head on his paws. We need an active dog. My husband wants a dog who can be a friend for our little boy. This dog sleeps all the time. He has no pep."

My heart went out to the puppy, who didn't even wriggle in the man's large hands. His tail drooped; he looked as hopeless as Stanwyck had after they had carted her father off to the court house.

"We'd like a credit. You said the dog was guaranteed. Perhaps a larger breed—maybe a retriever."

"You live in a four-room apartment?" the man asked.

"But we'd walk him," the woman said quickly. "That's the whole point. Get our little boy outside, away from the TV."

"This little fellow is going to grow. They're very active. That's why firemen keep them," he said shortly. Stroking the dog's head, he put him in one of the metal cages behind him. That woke the puppies who were sleeping in the cages on either side of the Dalmatian's. They stood up, yipped a few times, circled their cages, and collapsed again.

"Wonder if he drugs them?" Stanwyck whispered to me. "They all look limp."

The woman sighed. "If you get a real frisky dog in the next couple of weeks, would you give me a call? We're most anxious to get this whole dog business settled." Not waiting for a reply, she gathered up her gloves and hurried out of the store.

The man turned to us. "What'll it be, girls?"

"We're looking for a parrot—a real talky parrot?" Stanwyck asked, imitating the woman's high, nervous tone. The store owner didn't appreciate her wit.

"We don't carry parrots. Haven't for three years. Too expensive. Not enough call for them."

"You know of any parrot store nearby?" I asked.

"The best one in the country is old Monty Flyte's down in the West Village. But he's only open by appointment, and he's a serious bird handler. Monty wouldn't give the time of day to kids looking for a pet."

"We know what we're doing; this is no caged canary in the window we're after," Stan said, leaning across the counter and squinting up her face. "We've pooled all our Christmas money—about six hundred dollars. We want to start breeding parrots. Not all kids are airheads, you know."

"Maybe I could call Monty for you." He led us to the front of the store, away from the whining puppies. "If you want to leave me a deposit, I could probably get you a fine-quality talker in a few days' time."

"Could you give me your phone number?" Stanwyck asked smoothly. "I have to check out an African Gray with scarlet wings that I heard about uptown. If he doesn't pan out, I'll give you a call."

The man was clearly impressed. "You do know your birds! I'm sure I can do something for you." He reached into his breast pocket and handed Stanwyck a card. "I'm sorry if I sounded short with you. That wretched woman has returned three dogs to me since Christmas. Sometimes I think people should be required to be licensed to own pets."

"You'll be hearing from us," Stanwyck assured him.

As soon as we'd walked out of sight of the Dogeteria, Stanwyck looked down at her note pad. "Monty Flyte. West Village. Let's do it, Jess."

"Where in the West Village?"

27

"Wherever he is." Waving her arms to hail a cab, Stanwyck laughed. "Flyte, birds—this is going to be quite interesting."

I tugged at her sleeve. "Pretty awesome, that African Gray business!"

"Good thing I have total recall." A cab pulled up, and she opened the door. "Just a minute, sir, I have to check where we're going." Stan opened her bag and pulled out some folded, printed sheets of paper. "Phone book pages," she explained. "I did a little surgery on the pet store section."

"Oh, Stan, you shouldn't have!"

"Get serious, Jess. My father was taken away by the feds, remember?"

The cab driver turned around and gave us a very strange look.

"Rats," Stan said, scanning the pages. "There's no Flyte, no Monty's, no pet store in the West Village—except for Witty Kitty, that store near the subway that sells things in the shape of cats or with pictures of cats on them."

"Definitely not what we're looking for."

"You girls renting this cab as living space, or you want to travel somewhere?"

Stan gave her own address, and we returned to the loft. As we were getting out of the cab, I noticed a woman hurrying into the delivery entrance of the small building across the street. It was the gawky woman in the black raincoat. She was hard to forget, that long pale face with sagging cheeks and protruding teeth.

"Look, Stan, over there, that woman going into the building!"

"Where?" It was too late.

28

"It's the third time today I've noticed her. A real bow-wow. We might find her relatives in those small cages at the Dogeteria."

"No time for doggy women. We have to call Noah and get the crack code for the phone company information service."

"Stan, you're not going to start that business—not with the FBI swarming all over the loft!"

"We have to find Monty Flyte, and the reverse directory is the best way," she explained. We'd used the reverse directory when we were learning about the emergency 911 system. It's a computer listing of street addresses, building by building, and the phone numbers for each apartment or business. It allows you to find a number by street or full address if you don't have the name of the person. Phone operators only allow access to the reverse directory to people with legitimate reasons. So we'd have to crack into the system if we were going to snoop through the West Village streets to locate Monty Flyte.

Mrs. Baum had left us a note. The writing was slanted down the page, words were misspelled, and it was signed with a great, grinning face. Stanwyck's father was free on bail! There were so many questions to be answered that he'd gone immediately to a meeting at the lawyer's office. For the time being the feds were out of our hair. Exhausted from the day's drama, poor Mrs. B. was taking a nap.

The late afternoon sun slanted through the loft windows. While Stan went to the computer in her room, I sat with the print-out of phone calls to Brazil and Venezuela to see if I could discern any patterns.

About an hour passed. I covered several sheets of paper

with numbers, but I couldn't find any patterns. I even tried translating the numbers into letters, letting A be 1, B be 2, and so forth to see if they spelled out a secret message, but it was garbled nonsense. In her room Stanwyck was hunched over her computer, trying phreaker cracking codes. So far, she hadn't been able to break into the phone company's directory lines.

I wandered back to the window; the streetlights were on. In the little cul-de-sac, Terrapin Circle, that cuts through the block across the street from the Baums' loft, little kids were roller-skating. I watched as a little boy careened into the front door of one of the houses, screaming wildly. The houses on Terrapin Circle are national landmarks, all built about the time of the Revolutionary War. Filmmakers like to make movies there since the houses look the same as they did a hundred years ago. Even the streetlamps are antique. The brick-front houses are built directly onto the street, with no sidewalks or paths. My mom has often said that if she had a million dollars, she'd live on Terrapin Circle. There's an ornate iron gate that's locked at either end of the street at night to keep out traffic. When we were kids, Stan and I used to swing on the iron gates. Now they have a guard hired to keep out non-Terrapin people. When he first heard about the guard, Mel Baum huffed and puffed around the loft, insisting that locking us out of Terrapin Circle is unconstitutional. Since the mayor lives on Terrapin Circle, he's probably not going to do a lot about it.

I went back to Stanwyck's room. "Why not get Noah to phreak it out? He's faster than you are."

30

She looked hurt at the suggestion. "I taught him how to phreak."

"But you haven't been doing it. He's kept his hand in. Who cares which of us cracks the code? The goal is to find the real parrot smugglers, right?"

"Good old Jess. You call Noah; I'll keep running numbers here."

Good old Noah. He'd been running the phreak without Stanwyck's permission, and he had the code ready for me. "What timing! I was about to call her. It's three lines of code—simple, really. They've changed the entry numbers for the second password since we went in last time. That's what slowed me down. Now it's a five-digit number, with three at-signs and two asterisks before each carriage return. I've got the directory on my screen. Ask her if she wants me to download it or if she wants to enter from her own keyboard."

"Let you download it? Noah, you know Stanwyck! Give me the codes. She'll have to control it from here. But just in case something happens and Stanwyck can't get into their databank, capture the directory for the West Village on disk for me. She's screaming for the phone—I'll call if we need your disk."

The door opened and Mr. Baum walked in carrying an armload of papers. Embarrassed and at a loss as to what to say, I hurried into Stanwyck's room. "Your dad just walked through the door. I feel like a class-A jerk. What should I say to him?"

Stanwyck pushed past me. "Daddy!"

"A real pickle, huh, kids?" He smiled, but his eyes had

deep, dark circles under them. "Another couple of hours down there, and I would have confessed to using an inferior grade of down in our Excelsior top-of-the-line pillows."

"Did the feds hurt you, Daddy?" Stanwyck's voice was tiny and childlike. "Did they grill you under hot lights?"

"Get hold of yourself, Stanwyck. This is no TV show. I can't have you or your mother flipping out. There will be a bunch of lawyers coming over to review the case this evening, and you could be a big help if you'd go about your own life and leave the business of straightening out this mess to me and the professionals. Understood?"

Stanwyck smiled sweetly. "You're absolutely right, Daddy. Jess and I will go to an early movie, just like we'd planned all week. As soon as we've turned off the computer. Should we bring back Chinese for everybody?"

Chapter Three

"Of course we're not going to a movie. With my father headed for the slammer? We're going to meet Noah at The Coffee Pot and plan our strategy."

I wrapped my scarf more tightly around my neck. It was dinnertime. I was relieved that we'd got away from the loft before the news reports about Mr. Baum's arrest were broadcast. Even though it was vacation, my mother had not been too pleased at my vague promise to be home early. When she heard about the morning's drama, she'd be mega-irritated that I hadn't let her in on the story.

Without the sun, we were back into the bite of winter. "I don't want to walk all over the Village," I said as the wind almost carried my scarf away.

Stan threw her hand across my shoulder and said in her most cajoling tone, "You won't have to walk anywhere. We'll cab it to the Pot and wait inside for Noah. We're not going to look for Monty Flyte until we have become experts on birds." She hailed a cab, and we sped toward the East Village. As we crossed Sixth Avenue, I realized how tense things were at the loft.

"By the way, Noah's friend the Beak is coming with him. Noah says he's a touch weird—"

"*Noah* says he's weird?" I shook my head in disbelief. "Then the guy must not be in this galaxy! Noah's not exactly a walking advertisement for mental health week." We had met Noah through Stanwyck's computer bulletin board. He'd become so involved in interactive fantasy games that he'd convinced himself that he was involved in a life-and-death struggle with evil powers. "Fortunately, in the past few months he's spent more time in reality. I guess he can help us find this Flyte fellow."

Stanwyck bit her lip, trying to conceal her irritation.

"I'm sorry," I said after a few minutes of stiff silence. "I like Noah. I don't know why I said that."

"I wonder what people are saying about my father," Stanwyck said softly.

I paid the driver, and we found a booth in the back of The Coffee Pot, where we settled in to wait for Noah and the Beak. I got wired on three cups of coffee before they showed up. Looking like a comedy team, they headed toward our table. Short, dark Noah, who always walks looking at the ground, was followed by a very tall boy who reminded me of an upended broom. He had spiky blond hair that fanned out behind his ears and stuck out from his forehead. He had very long arms that he held in triangles to his body. His sharp elbows narrowly missed knocking a platter of fries out of a waitress's hand. His backpack slammed into a coat rack, scattering a couple of down jackets. Unconcerned, he kept on walking; his pale eyes blinked out from odd-shaped half-glasses. He looked like the sort of person Stanwyck might have invented to cheer herself up.

Noah sat down opposite me, and his friend flopped down next to him. The Beak set his backpack down on my feet. I kicked it back to his side of the table. He didn't seem to notice. Sitting, he was as tall as the waitress who came to take our order. Stan outlined what we knew of the case against her father.

"Parrot smuggling's not news," the Beak said. "Been going on for years. Collectors and aviculturists justify smuggling out rare species by claiming that they'll breed up their numbers, so they're actually protecting the species. Of course, nobody considers whether the bird is happier in its own jungle in Panama or in somebody's tacky aviary in southern California."

"Let's not get into birds' rights," Stan said hastily. "We need to find the real smugglers so we can clear my dad. Do you want to help?"

"By the way, Beak, there was a real squirrelly guy at the press conference who dumped the feathers. Did you see him on the news? He's from one of those organizations to save birds," I said.

"I belong to the Feather Society and to Downwind," he told me. "Neither of them would pull such a grandstand play as dumping feathers for TV cameras."

Noah pulled a computer print-out from his pocket. "These are the phone company entry codes for the new NYNEX system. They're longer, but they're basically as easy to crack as the old Ma Bell patterns were. See? They use female first

35

names, followed by three nonalphanumerics in keyboard sequence."

"I don't see that," I muttered. But I had never been able to sort out the patterns that seemed so obvious to Noah and Stanwyck.

"I had time to print out the reverse directory only for the streets south of Bleecker and west of Greenwich Avenue. And I don't see any Flyte or bird store or pet store. Could it be under any other name?"

"You ever hear of a parrot dealer named Monty Flyte?" I asked the Beak.

He leaned across the table at me until his face was almost touching my onion rings. "I don't keep birds in cages. I'm not a prison guard."

"Now, Beak," Stanwyck said, seizing his bony wrist, "we don't have time for mini free-the-birds sermons every time one of us asks you a question. Please try to control your birdiness."

He grinned good-naturedly. "It's how I am. Always have been. I identify with birds. When I was four, I refused to eat eggs. Still won't handle an egg. As I see it, egg cartons are bird coffins. My folks have sent me to shrinks and aviary specialists. Everyone tries to assure me that birds don't care if they're caged and that it protects them from predators and that commercial chicken eggs aren't fertilized. Everybody fills me full of information, but nobody has ever succeeded in convincing me to swallow potential birds, which is what eggs are. If everyone stopped eating eggs, chickens would be able to repopulate in peace."

"The world would be overrun with chickens," said Noah.

"City playgrounds would have hordes of wild chickens playing in the sandboxes and strutting across the benches, fighting with the pigeons for air space."

"The shrinks think I wish I were a bird. Which is ridiculous. I have more freedom as a person. I've never wanted to be a bird. What I would like to be is a human being who could fly. Best of both worlds, you know?"

He does move his arms like wings, I thought to myself. But I didn't want to fuel his birdy talk any longer. "Stan's right. We have very little time to get info on the real smugglers if we're going to help her father."

Stanwyck leaned across the table. "The way I figure it, we need to investigate two areas. Certainly we have to find out who the real parrot smugglers are," she said eagerly. "But we also have to convince the feds that the list of phone calls is computer-generated. With great pain, I admit that it looks like the work of phreakers. That's where I think you'd be most helpful, Noah. You still in touch with most of those bulletin-board friends of yours?"

Noah ducked his head and ate in silence for a few minutes. Finally, he met Stanwyck's patient gaze. "I still cruise the boards. But I haven't been in touch with the Dungeon Master, not since—"

Stanwyck shook her head. "I know. You promised, and you've been faithful."

"How do you know?" I asked.

"I check the games from time to time to make sure Noah's password isn't among the players." She winked at Noah. "Not that I don't trust you. But I know how tempting the old games can be. Those little symbols filling up the screen.

Some days I long to be a sysop again. Nobody ever will run as great a BBS as I did."

Noah turned to the Beak. "If only you'd known her then, Beak! She was the rarest bird! She ran the greatest BBS that ever was on-line."

"What does that have to do with parrots?" The Beak looked at my coleslaw with interest. I handed him the plate. He finished it in a few forkfuls.

"Background," Stanwyck said crisply. "You're not working with amateurs."

"What can I do to help? Noah knows I don't have any computer facility."

"It's the bird knowledge. You and Jess will go to pet stores— "

"I would never enter an institution of animal sales!" he said, clamping his lips together like a little kid refusing medicine. "Members of Downwind take a pledge never to keep a bird in captivity."

The waitress cleared away our plates and brought us fresh Cokes. "You could do the behind-the-scenes research. Teach me about birds so I'll sound convincing to the pet-store people," I suggested. "You wouldn't have to compromise your principles."

He disappeared under the table and struggled with his backpack. Then his upper body reappeared. He handed me a couple of books with bright green and yellow parrots on their covers. "This ought to do the trick. These books give the rudiments of parrot culture. Not much on the care of diseased birds, but you'll be able to identify species and talk about their basic care and feeding."

Noah had been studying the lists of phone calls charged to Mr. Baum's office. I noticed that he still wrote figures with a ball-point pen on the backs of his hands when he was trying to crack codes and patterns. His lips moved, silently mouthing numbers as he worked. His involvement seemed to comfort Stanwyck as nothing else had all day. "It's definitely a phreak," he pronounced a few minutes later. "You can tell that a computer's been set to dial a certain number of calls per hour to these numbers in Rio, then to Bahia, then to this Venezuela town. The reason the calls are logged in every few minutes is that the computer hangs up as soon as the connection is completed. It's the sort of phreak people use when they're bleeding toll numbers."

"Whatever are you talking about?" I asked.

"You know those our-operators-are-standing-by ads on TV?" Noah asked. "Well, you set the computer to call the 800 number every four minutes and hang up as soon as the connection is completed. The company with the 800 number gets charged for the call the same as if you had ordered the record albums or the collection of thimbles or whatever garbage."

"What's the point of the phreak?"

"If you set the computer to make twenty calls an hour for thirty hours, the company is charged more than six hundred dollars. If ten people phreak the number for a month, we're talking about seventy-five thousand dollars. A nice piece of change. I heard on TV of one scam where one of those fundamentalist preachers had been charged with almost half a million dollars in phony charges. They didn't mention phreakers, but I thought to myself, behind that scam lies a very radical phreak. I'd like to meet that phreaker!" He sighed.

"Now, you promised, Noah," I warned, then looked away. "Sorry for sounding like your local parents' committee."

"But why Brazil?" Stanwyck asked. "Why not Philadelphia? It must be expensive to dial Brazil."

"It's a new twist. Whoever's masterminding the phreak has an admirably phreaky mind," Noah said. "The 800 company gets charged at least twice as much for calls logged from outside the continental U.S. Now with satellite-dish TV, programs are beamed all around the hemisphere, including the ads. That's why some of the 800 ads tell people in Alaska and Hawaii to call collect to a non-800 number. Merchandisers are afraid of losing too much money with those double-rate assessments."

"And the phreaker's phone bill is phreaked into another number anyway. That explains how my father's involved," Stanwyck said. "How could I not have seen the setup?"

"It must be twice as satisfying to phreak internationally," Noah said.

"We never got to do that." Stanwyck frowned. "I wonder if we should try—just to see if your scenario really plays."

"No way! We could be in reform school." I reminded her of the judge's warning after our last caper.

"Curious that nobody's hooked onto the 800 scam yet," Stanwyck said, tracing the number *800* on the table with the point of her fork.

"I haven't heard of any arrests," Noah said, catching her eye. "Maybe we should run a test scam as a way to attract the real phreakers to us."

"I'll squeal. I'll turn state's evidence. I'll buy ads in the newspapers," I said desperately.

"Let's not get all atwitter." The Beak blinked at me. "They're trying to get your goat, old girl."

What's he looking so smug for? I thought. I glared at the Beak, but he seemed oblivious to my irritation.

"Have you ever been to the Hall of Night at the Bronx Zoo?" he asked.

"Calm down, Jess. You know how long it takes the feds to get onto a scam. First they have to learn about the crack, then they have to draft legislation, then they have to pass the law—it's a good six months between the time of the first appearance of a dynamite crack and the time the feds move to kill it." Stanwyck sighed comically. "As I know all too well."

The Beak stretched his arms over his head. He seemed to be itching to move. "All that phreaking energy could be put to good use. Like liberating animals and birds from zoos."

"Could we have our check, please?" I called to the waitress.

Reluctantly, the Beak agreed to meet us at the loft the following morning at noon. As we walked Noah to the subway, it was clear that he was pleased to be back in Stanwyck's orbit. I'd forgotten how solitary his life was, since his father worked at the university library until midnight every night. Too bad it had taken this crisis to bring Noah back into our lives.

Not surprisingly, my parents were waiting in the living room. "What's going on with Mel Baum? Were the news reports correct?" Mom was knitting the sleeve of a sweater she was making for me. It was a lovely shade of mauve. I'd

41

picked out the wool myself. After the events of the past twenty-four hours, I suspected the sweater would always remind me of parrots and Mr. Baum's troubles.

I told the story, omitting the fact that Stan and I were planning to produce the real smugglers and uncover the phone phreakers. "Clearly he's been framed. Mr. Baum wouldn't do anything illegal."

"The government doesn't usually make arrests until they have a pretty good case," my father remarked quietly. "They have evidence that they believe will stand up in court."

Mom cleared her throat. "You should be prepared, Jess. Sometimes people let us down."

"I can't believe you guys!"

"Everything isn't always what it seems. And if Mel Baum has been trafficking in stolen birds, poor Stanwyck will need your friendship more than ever."

"You don't think he's guilty!" I exclaimed.

"It's a possibility—that's all your father is saying." Mother never broke the rhythm of her knitting. I was amazed at how they could sit in their usual chairs in our living room and say such outrageous things about my best friend's father without the slightest evidence of emotion.

I settled for a quick "you can't be serious" and went off to my room. The next morning I was out of the house before they were up. I didn't leave a note; it was obvious where they could find me.

When I got off the train in Stan's neighborhood, I decided to take the shortcut through Terrapin Circle. For the first time, I noticed a bronze plaque mounted on the massive brick column into which the gates were set. It read:

TERRAPIN CIRCLE: THE FOUR ORIGINAL HOUSES WERE BUILT FOR
NORTON ELIOT MADISON AND HIS THREE SONS IN 1792. THE TWO
HOUSES AT THE NORTH END OF THE CIRCLE WERE ADDED IN 1825
FOR LYDIA AND LETITIA MADISON AS WEDDING PRESENTS FROM
THEIR FATHER, COMMANDER THEODORE POLLARD MADISON. A
DESCENDANT OF THE MADISON FAMILY HAS LIVED IN THE CIRCLE
SINCE THE FIRST HOUSES WERE BUILT.

The morning sun was not yet high enough in the sky to
lighten the foreboding quality of the deserted street. The
windows of the six houses that make up the Circle were
heavily curtained. The street had been swept clean; there
was no garbage or litter in sight. The place had the forced
reality of the phony "historic" streets at Disney World.

I wondered which of the houses the current descendant of
the Madison family lived in. The heavy chains that held the
tall, wrought-iron gates locked at night were dangling from
the bars of the gates. Somebody must get up and open them
early every morning, I thought. Although the gates were
unlocked, I had to push against one of the heavy gates to
gain entrance to the Circle. They might have been techni-
cally unlocked, but they sure didn't make it easy for visitors.
I looked over my shoulder as I walked down the silent
street, feeling like a trespasser. I half expected someone to
open one of those blank windows and yell at me to leave.
This is ridiculous, I reminded myself. You are walking along
a public street. You're not in someone's driveway. I glanced
up at each doorway as I passed it, imagining what it had
been like almost two hundred years ago, when all those
brothers and sisters raised their children there and no one
ever left home.

As I approached the iron gates at the other end of the Circle, the door of the second house from the corner opened. I looked up. It was the tall dark woman I'd seen from the window of the Baums' loft the day before. She was wearing her shapeless black raincoat. She'd started down the steps when she caught sight of me, paused for a moment, turned, and dashed back up the stairs and inside her house. But she didn't slam the door; she closed it gently behind her, as if taking great care not to hurt the door or the doorpost or the thick morning silence, as heavy as fog, that covered the Circle.

Stanwyck would expect a complete description of the mystery woman. As I walked down the block toward the loft, I spoke under my breath, glad there was no one on the street to overhear me: "She had the palest skin, as if her blood had been drained away in the night. Bare, stick-shaped legs and bony ankles poked out from under her coat. Her green brocade slippers were too large for her bony feet. They slapped the steps as she ran."

"Mom's in bed; not sleeping, merely lying there comatose. I brought her tea. She let it get cold. I brought her some more, and she's still staring at the ceiling," Stan reported as soon as I entered the loft. "Dad went out to buy the papers. Might as well face the music. He's got guts," she said with admiration. "I heard them talking late into the night. I don't think any of us slept much."

"No new developments?" I asked. Stanwyck did not seem in the mood to hear about the weird woman from Terrapin Circle. "I figured Noah would have the phreak cracked by now."

44

"I thought he might, too. You know he never shuts down the computer before four in the morning. First thing when I woke up, I checked my computer to see if he'd downloaded anything to me during the night. But it's a blank."

"You think we have the right gig? That it's an organized international 800 crack?"

"Got to be." She squeezed my hand. "If I'm right, we haven't seen the worst. There'll be hundreds more of these calls charged to Dad. And they could be made from anywhere in the Western Hemisphere. After what Noah said last night, I've been wondering if maybe the phreaker scam might not be based in Brazil. I mean, after all, they have kids there as smart as we are, don't you think?"

"But calls booked now would prove your dad's innocence!" I insisted.

She looked at me quizzically.

"Don't you see?" I said excitedly. "If there are calls made after yesterday, it will be obvious that your dad didn't make them. It will be clear that someone is using his number."

Stanwyck sighed. "They already think he's guilty. They'll figure it's his accomplices making the calls, warning the South American connections. Once they've made up their minds, all evidence gets interpreted through guilty lenses. We've got to uncover the genuine phreakers to clear Daddy's name." She spun around on her chair. "I hope they're wizards. Maybe we can even learn from them."

"Get serious, Stan. After what they're doing to your dad? They're pond scum, roadfill!"

The phone rang. We let it ring a few times to see if Mrs. Baum would answer it. "Hello?" Stanwyck said tentatively.

Her face was glowing as if it were the mythical South American accomplices. "Drop dead, you turkey!" she shouted a moment later, and slammed down the receiver.

"What was that all about?" I asked.

We heard the key in the lock. Mr. Baum opened the door; his arms were filled with newspapers.

"Hello, Daddy. Can I fix you some toast or a muffin?" Stan's voice was higher than usual and artifically sweetened.

"I'm not terminally ill, girls. Don't treat me as if you expect me to croak before sundown." He plunked the papers onto the kitchen counter and lit the cigar that was dangling from his mouth. "We'll get through this business." He gestured to the papers. "When your mother sees these, she'll be convinced she can never go outside this loft again. Let's try to play down the drama, if you get my drift."

As if on cue, Mrs. Baum appeared in the doorway wrapped in a shawl. "I can't even remember ordinary life, where you take a shower and get dressed and go shopping on a Saturday morning." She shuddered and pulled her shawl more tightly around her shoulders.

I hurried to the front window to get away from Mrs. Baum's look of fear. For the first time, I was struck by the seriousness of the situation. I felt like an intruder, embarrassed at my excitement and interest, as if it were a TV cop show and not the real person I knew being sent to an actual prison, not some TV jail with phony bars.

A moment later Stanwyck joined me. "Dad's right. She's losing it. By lunchtime, she'll be a basket case. Let's get out of here."

"Where do you want to go?" I asked.

46

"Anywhere. Before she attaches herself to me and we're trapped here all day. You know she gets very clingy when there's trouble. Remember how she came apart like a cheap umbrella that time when Noah disappeared? She was worse than Noah's father!"

As I looked at the street, something clicked. "Stanwyck, why was she carrying a plastic trash bag when there are no garbage cans on the street of Terrapin Circle?"

Stanwyck smacked her forehead. "It's contagious. You're all bonkers. Who was carrying a trash bag? My mother never carries the trash downstairs—even when she's not singing the Hill Street Blues."

"Girls, if your father comes back, tell him I'm lying down."

"Mom, he's right behind you. Reading the papers!"

Mrs. Baum turned around as if to prove Stanwyck wrong. "Mel, don't sit there so quietly. I didn't know you were there."

"I should tap-dance, with all the trouble I have?"

I pulled Stanwyck back to the window. "I am on to something major. We have to investigate Terrapin Circle. The spooky woman in the black raincoat—I saw her this morning in Terrapin Circle. Plus, yesterday she was standing in the doorway of the building across the street while the news people were here. Then I saw her later going into the service entrance of that same building. And this morning she was coming out of a house on Terrapin Circle." I paused until I had Stanwyck's full attention.

"You have a point with all this?" Stanwyck chewed her lip.

"She had a full trash bag, but there are no trash cans near her house."

Stanwyck shook her head in exasperation. "Jess, if you're going to be any help in this investigation, you've got to stop seeing criminals sneaking out of every door. Rounding up every New Yorker who has a full bag of trash is not going to take the heat off my father."

"Make fun of me! But that woman looked guilty as hell. Her mouth quivered when she saw me. She ran back upstairs and took the trash back inside with her. Is that the act of a normal person dumping garbage?"

"A mystery woman in a black raincoat." Stanwyck sighed. "It's almost too good to be true."

Chapter Four

Stanwyck hailed a cab as soon as we got to the street. "Where are we going?" I asked. Fleeing the loft in a cab was becoming routine.

"Where to, girls?" the driver demanded. A pair of purple furry dice were hanging from his rearview mirror. Pictures of children in ornate plastic frames were mounted across the dashboard. A shag rug in shades of purple covered the back of the cab. "This is how the Brothers Grimm would have decorated the witch's cottage if Hansel and Gretel had been old enough to drive," I whispered to Stanwyck. On an ordinary day she would have laughed.

"Main library on Forty-second Street," said Stanwyck, as if I hadn't spoken.

"Sounds like fun," I grumbled.

"It will be. When we leave, we'll know more about raising parrots than most people. Certainly as much as that clown in the pet store yesterday."

As we ran up the flights of steep steps to the main entrance of the library, I saw a familiar figure. "Stan, look! The Beak!"

Sure enough, a little to the left of the main doors, the Beak stood. He was grinning darkly and was clasping a half-empty cardboard container of cocoa. "Knew you'd pick the wrong library! Knew you'd pick it this morning!"

Stanwyck nudged his pack, setting him slightly off balance. "This is the largest library in the country, probably in the whole world. What's wrong about it?"

"Parrots," he said, as if he were being charged by the word. "It's not known for its collection on parrot culture." He scanned the cloudless sky. "Wide-open air! The power of wings, the softness of feathers."

Stanwyck sat on the steps, away from the flow of people hurrying into the library. "My father's looking at a life sentence if we have to depend on this geek."

The Beak raised his long arms. "The more you watch birds fly, the more you hear their songs in your mind."

"Sit down, please." I touched his arm lightly. For a moment I almost believed he could fly away from us.

He blinked cheerfully and sat down; his bony knees rose up close to his chin. "Have you ever examined a flight feather closely? It's perfectly designed so that when pressure is put on it, no air can pass through it. A miracle."

"Feathers!" I reached into my jacket pocket and pulled out a handful of the feathers that had been dumped on the ground during the press conference.

Shielding the bright feathers from the wind with his torso, the Beak turned them over in his hand. "These blue and black ones are flights. And these long green ones with the bluish tinge are upper tail. These dull fuzzy ones are from a female, probably a young one."

"How can you tell?"

"Bright silky plumage is male; it's how they attract for breeding."

"Like rock stars," remarked Stanwyck. "Can you tell if they're from parrots?"

"Not for certain. But they're about the right size for parrots. I'd say they're from molting birds. If it's an aviary, somebody's got a flock of sick birds. Because parrots usually molt in the summer months. Although I don't know what happens to parrots living in captivity."

"If only we could find Monty Flyte." I put the feathers into my pocket.

"Did you say Flyte?" The Beak blinked a few times. "There's a Flyte who's curator of birds at the Museum of Natural History. But he'd never sell imprisoned birds. He's got integrity. He's a lifetime director of the Feather Society. Won their gold feather a few years ago. I worked for him last summer, cataloging slides from his last jungle trip. It was quite an honor."

Stan gathered new energy from this information. "What are we waiting for? Would he be working today? Can you take us to him?"

"He practically lives at the museum. He wouldn't remember to eat if someone didn't put food in front of him."

"Jungle trips, huh? This is the first encouraging sign we've had." I clapped the Beak on the back. "*He* may be the real connection."

"Things couldn't fall into place this easily," Stanwyck said

51

with more than her usual share of caution. "If bird smugglers could be easily traced, why wouldn't the feds have found the real crooks?"

"Because they already have it in their minds that it is your dad. Remember what you said about phone phreaks? Well, it's probably the same with the smugglers."

The Beak shook his head angrily. "You're really off the wall. Dr. Flyte wouldn't be involved in trapping birds. He's the best friend a bird could have—especially in this city, where people would rather wear feathers and furs than respect the creatures who rightfully own them."

I remembered rooms full of stuffed birds perched on tree branches behind glass windows at the museum, but I didn't want to get the Beak any more wound up than he already was.

About an hour later, we were climbing twisted flights of stairs into one of the high stone towers of the museum. All the guards seemed to know the Beak. They waved us through door after door that said NO ADMITTANCE. We must have walked half a mile through poorly lit back corridors. The Beak hummed under his breath. Stan and I were silent. Finally we were standing in front of a dark green door with a typed card thumbtacked at eye level: WINSTON FLYTE.

"It must be the same guy we heard about yesterday. No wonder he wasn't listed in the phone book. What a great cover for a bird operation—a museum. Beak, you're a genius," Stanwyck said, a tear on her eyelashes.

Without knocking or calling out, the Beak went into the room. He looked around happily. "Great place!" He motioned to a large worktable under the windows. "In the summer, when the trees outside are in full bloom, it's like a nest." He went to the door of an inner room and cleared his throat. "Dr. Flyte, it's Beak. I've brought some friends."

The walls were lined with dark wooden cabinets with glass fronts. Each cabinet was filled with birds. The one directly in front of us held bluejays and robins and other common birds. I turned sharply toward the part of the room that was in shadow. Seeing familiar birds made me uneasy. They seemed so alive, so ready to be birds again. Fortunately, the other cabinets stood in the shadows; there was just a glimmer of an iridescent feather where light shone into the cabinet.

An immaculate man in a spotless white jacket came to the door. He looked like a TV doctor about to recommend cough medicine that would unblock your sinuses while allowing you to sleep all night. "How nice, Beak!" He peered at us. "Girls!"

"That's right." The Beak seemed pleased. "They need to know about parrots. One of them—her father, that is—has been accused of smuggling parrots. You know anything about black-market birds?"

He shook his head. His gray hair had the sheen of feathers. "Only what I read in the papers."

"We didn't expect he'd admit it straightaway," I whispered to Stan.

"Beak shouldn't call them black-market birds." Stanwyck sat on a backless stool and leaned her elbows on the worktable. "Makes it seem like we're looking for crooks. My dad is in some trouble, and we thought if we could buy a spectacular parrot, it would take my mom's mind off the lawyers and the media swarming around the apartment. You understand."

He smoothed the stubby gray hairs on his moustache. "Birds are a great comfort," he agreed. "But, my dear, the only birds I have are dead. Being prepared for exhibits—don't you see?"

"The doctor would never cage live birds," the Beak assured us.

Wonder how he kills them? I thought, reminding myself to discuss this with Stanwyck after we'd left the Beak.

"We need your expertise," Stan continued. "You see, we've been told by several sources that you are el primo parrot dealer in New York. We don't pay attention to the Beak's nonsense. Selling birds is perfectly legal. It's actually a service to those who want to protect endangered species, to breed up their numbers." Stan had found time to read a few pages in those books of the Beak's.

"Who could have told you I deal in parrots?" he mused.

Stanwyck shot me a glance that said "Don't volunteer any more information." The Beak went into the inner room, leaving us alone with Dr. Flyte.

He fiddled with a stack of slides on his desk, as if trying to make up his mind about something. "There's my brother," he began slowly. "Monty Flyte. But he's a bit of an odd duck. Doesn't like people much. Probably wouldn't agree to see you. He works with aviculturists—as you say, to help keep the dwindling species out of danger. And of course there's Felicity Licht. But she'd never sell one of her birds. Got one of her old Eclectus Parrots on the bench now. Waiting for the right tint of eyes before we finish her off."

He called over his shoulder to the Beak to bring out the Eclectus on the stretching frame.

"Isn't it a beauty?" the Beak asked, cradling the dead bird in his cupped hands. "Look, Jess," he said, noticing that I had closed my eyes as he and the bird approached, "the color pattern of the beak looks like candy corn."

"No, no, that's the male." Dr. Flyte laughed gently. "How could you forget such a thing, Beak?" He disappeared into the other room and returned with a second bird. There were no feathers on its left side. One wing was hanging by silk threads a few inches from its body. I walked toward the door, hoping the feeling of nausea would subside.

Oblivious to my discomfort, the birdman continued like a tape recorder. "The female has the most delightful feathers. Soft as fine fur. The wings are deep maroon. The underwings are shaded with blue, maroon, and green at the upper end that extends to the black shading of the flight feathers. The vent is red. The underside of the tail—"

"We get the idea," Stanwyck said, making a great effort to stay on the near side of polite. "Very lovely birds. Where can we find Felicity?"

"Oh, she avoids people more than my brother. Compared with Felicity, Monty's a man-about-town." He smiled at me, still holding the flimsy parrot. "But her awkwardness around people's not the issue. Poor soul. Felicity has one of the finest private aviaries in the Western Hemisphere, and yet she's too frightened to share those exquisite birds with anyone."

I glanced at the Beak, expecting one of his free-the-birds outbursts, but he sat listening as if it were a movie of the week.

"Where does she get her birds?" Stanwyck asked.

"There are sources," he said vaguely. "She's known all over the world. People send her specimens, hoping she'll agree to take on a particularly rare bird. She's very generous. When she loses a rare baby, she sends it to me. Like these Eclecti—some of the finest specimens. You simply don't see birds like this in domestic conditions. Felicity's got a true gift. This pair was from the South Pacific Islands. They're called Sacred Temple Parrots because they've been the object of worship in native religious rites."

"Is her aviary near the city?" I asked to break the spell of bird talk.

"Near the city?" he laughed, clearly delighted. "It's in the city. She's spared no expense. Converted her whole house into a series of aviaries. Of course, it's quite hush-hush. If anyone knew, she'd be prey to robbers. The birds wouldn't be safe." He shook his head. "I have to protect her privacy. For the sake of the parrots."

To my utter surprise, Stanwyck began to weep. "My father has one foot in jail, and you're worried about protecting birds! Who's going to protect my innocent father?" I tried to comfort her, but the taps had been turned on. The Beak dashed around the room, opening cabinets, peering inside, closing the doors again.

"What exactly did her father do, or not do?" Dr. Flyte asked me in a low tone. He seemed hesitant, as if his choice of words might send me into tears, too. With my arm around Stanwyck, patting her hair, I explained about the reporters and the trash bags of feathers that had been found outside the loft. "And the clincher seems to be these phone calls to Rio and Bahia and Venezuela that were charged to his office. Hundreds of calls. Although Stan and I are convinced that phone phreakers made the calls to crack the 800-number codes."

"Whatever for?" he stroked his moustache.

"As a challenge." I shrugged. "Phreakers look at things differently. If they see a toll-free number, it doesn't mean free access to a product or information. It sets up a challenge. A game between them and the authorities. Write a code programming the computer to dial the number twenty times an hour, for example, for a period of thirty hours. Then you get all the members of your phreaker board to do the same thing and see how many thousands of calls you can pile up."

Stan looked up, her cheeks wet with tears. "If my father hadn't been trapped by it, I'd think it was a capital phreak myself. I'd envy the guys who thought it up."

Whatever advantage we'd gained by the tears had just been lost. I pinched her arm to stop the true confessions. "You know, I understand the Parrot Woman's desire for privacy. And your brother's, too. But wouldn't they rather talk to Stan and me, two kids, than have federal agents swarming all over the aviary? They might even impound some of her birds. They might think her parrots are evidence."

"They'd have no cause," Dr. Flyte said, but his eyes showed fear.

"They had no cause to arrest Stan's father. Circumstantial evidence. Bags of feathers outside his house. Could have

57

been dumped there by anyone. They're on the lookout for parrot smugglers from Brazil. If she's got Brazilian birds—"

"Of course she's got Brazilian birds. The majority of her conures are from Brazil." He went into the inner room shaking his head.

Stan jumped up and threw her arms around me. "You're a genius. Cagney and Lacey couldn't have applied pressure more effectively. Awesome, Jess!"

"It even convinced me," I admitted. "Suddenly I feared for those defenseless parrots, with the feds dropping them into plastic bags."

Stan began to giggle. "How do you handcuff a parrot?"

"Or read him his rights?"

The Beak slammed the cabinet door. "That's not funny!"

Dr. Flyte reappeared in the doorway. "If you girls will meet me at ten tomorrow morning, Miss Felicity Licht will answer your questions." He handed me a folded piece of paper. "Here's the address." He seemed to have lost his starch. "I hope I'm doing the right thing."

"Free the parrots!" exclaimed the Beak. "That's the right thing."

There seemed no point in inviting him to go to the aviary with us.

Two young men sat at the kitchen counter with Mr. Baum. Several temporary telephones had been installed. One of the young men was talking to an overseas operator and taking notes on a pad. There were thick stacks of yellow paper on every surface. A copy of the list of phone calls to Brazil was taped to the refrigerator door. A third young man was setting up a tape recorder on the low table in the living room. Stacks of ledgers from the mattress factory were lined up on the couch.

"Where's Mom?" Stanwyck asked, nibbling a bagel chip from the bowl in front of her father.

"She's still in bed. Maybe you can rouse her." He poured himself a diet cola. "Giving up is never the ticket. We're going to beat this thing." He sounded like a sports coach trying to convince a very clumsy bunch of players that victory was in the bag.

"I'm Jess Graham," I said to the fellow who was adjusting knobs on the tape recorder. I tossed my coat on top of some of the ledgers on the couch and sat down in the chair closest to him.

"I'm Ray Brown. Assistant to Mr. Sheldon. We all work in some division of Danser Whippiny. Lou Gadamer and I joined the firm two years ago, but I've been in California on an antitrust case for the past three months. I work in litigation."

"What's that?" I liked his quick smile.

"I'm a trial lawyer. I argue cases in court most of the time." He grinned. "Where the action is."

"Aren't all lawyers in court?"

"Most lawyers never see the inside of a courtroom. Those guys across the room work for the firm's trust and estate division. When Mr. Baum called Mr. Sheldon, they recruited people for the case from various divisions of the firm. It seemed to me like a very interesting case. I've never done criminal work before. It's a great opportunity—one you never expect to get in a Wall Street firm."

"Glad someone is getting some benefit from this mess," I remarked. "So you guys all work together?"

"Not exactly. I've never even met the redhead, Thomas, before. He must be a new recruit. He met me and Lou downstairs this morning. Said he'd been sent by Mr. Sheldon to help with the paperwork."

I glanced over to the kitchen area. Mr. Baum was rubbing his eyes. "Poor man. He looks exhausted."

"Case is shaping up pretty grim," admitted Ray. "Unless we can convince the prosecutors that there's another smuggler controlling a major importing operation with heavy Brazil and Venezuela connections, well, your Mr. Baum's going to stand trial."

"Don't say anything to the other folks"—I stretched out my legs on the low table in front of the couch—"but Stanwyck and I are following a hot lead. We have a tip on a new international phone phreak, and it may bear fruit tomorrow."

He laughed. "Teenage investigators! I feel safer already."

"Don't be so high and mighty!" I looked at him without disguising my dislike. "It wasn't so long ago that you were my age, Mr. Litigator Brown."

"And I solved many a fascinating case." He flashed that smug smile.

"You're a detective?" Stanwyck came out from her mother's bedroom in time to overhear his last statement.

"No, he couldn't find his own shoes if they were on his feet. And he doesn't think we're any better."

Stanwyck nodded. "Let him think that, Jess. It'll keep him out of our hair." She turned to Ray Brown. "Don't wind up

60

your case till you check with us. We'll have the witnessess you need to free my father before the case ever comes to trial."

"Want to bet a steak on it, ladies?"

"Start saving your money," I warned him.

"I like mine medium rare. With well-done fries." Stanwyck grabbed our coats, and we went into her room to check on Noah's progress.

"Nothing on the computer. And he hasn't answered his phone all day. His dad is probably at the library. I don't know what Noah's up to."

I put my hands in my jeans pocket in imitation of Ray Brown. " 'Teenage invest-i-gators.' He makes the word sound like *all-i-gators*. What a snot!"

"An adorable snot," Stanwyck said as she dialed Noah's phone number. "When you like someone, Jess, you're as subtle as a perfume ad."

There were loud shouts from the dining room. Stan dropped the phone, and we ran inside. One of the research guys was jumping around the kitchen. "Now we're getting somewhere! I got hold of a fellow I went to college with. He works in Caracas as a stringer for one of the Boston papers. He did some checking for us. This number in Caracas is a movie theater that hasn't shown any films in three months, and this other Caracas number is a meat-packing plant that was nationalized last year."

"Good work, Lou. This weakens their case." The other one, Thomas, clapped him on the back. "Brown, why don't you try tracing the numbers in Bahia? I'm not having much luck with the Rio numbers. There seems to be no pattern."

61

Ray Brown pulled one of the phones toward him.

"There's no pattern because they're computer-generated," began Stanwyck.

"Now, honey, let's bottle that phreaker talk. We're paying these guys by the hour. Don't interrupt them." Mr. Baum rubbed his temples. "My eyes are burning. Think I'll throw some cold water on my face. Good work, Lou."

Stanwyck and I went back to her room. "We have to solve it now, Jess. I'm tired of being treated like a stuffed toy." She flipped on the computer. The screen remained blank. "And where is that idiot Noah!"

"Don't turn on Noah," I said, stuffing my hands into my pockets once again. "He's a teenage invest-i-gator." I pulled a piece of paper from my pocket. On it was the address Dr. Flyte had given me. Opening it, I gasped and fell onto Stanwyck's bed. "Look!" I whispered, shaking the paper in her face.

"Miss Felicity Licht, 2 Terrapin Circle, at the corner of Spring Street." Stanwyck looked at me wide-eyed. "Across the street!"

"It's the woman in the black raincoat, I'm sure of it. Now will you believe she's mega-weird?"

"The trash bag was probably stuffed with dead parrots," said Stanwyck darkly.

"You owe me a humongous apology. Remember, I fingered her."

"Now that I think about it, I know I've seen that pale woman skulking around the neighborhood in a dark raincoat. I forgot in the confusion of Daddy's arrest." Stanwyck thumped her pillow against the wall. "We've got to keep the Circle under surveillance."

"I think we ought to leave that to those geniuses—Gadamer and Brown—that your father's hired."

"You heard Dad. They get paid by the hour."

"Let them stand out in the cold, and we can make the calls to Brazil in the warmth of the kitchen," I suggested.

Without a word, Stanwyck stood over me, holding out my coat.

Chapter Five

"Do you know what Noah's doing?"

"Probably sleeping." I squinted across the street at Terrapin Circle, which was as still as a painting. "It's not even eight o'clock, and it's Sunday."

Stanwyck bit into a chocolate doughnut. "You're grumbling more than usual these days, Jess. Either it's too cold or too early, or you don't want to walk three blocks—"

"It is cold, and it's way too early. The sun is still asleep. But I'm here, ready to catch the Parrot Woman when she smuggles some birds out under that dreary black raincoat. So let's not start biting at each other." I thought of the Parrot Woman's concave body and long legs. Her sharp-featured face was birdlike. I couldn't imagine her collecting shaggy dogs who climb all over you and lick your face, bursting with sentiment. "People are attracted to animals who are like them."

"What do you mean?" Stanwyck poured some cocoa from a bright red Thermos and handed me the cup of steaming liquid. "This ought to make you a bit sweeter. I thought of everything," she said, reaching into her pocket for a small plastic bag. She dropped a few tiny marshmallows into my cup. "Details—that's the bottom line. You work through all the details, and the whole picture becomes clear."

"You have any trouble getting out of the house so early?" I asked.

"None. They have no idea that we're closing in on Felicity Licht this morning. Subtlety is my middle name. In other words, they were asleep."

"Mine were, too. So I postponed the inquisition for another day."

Stanwyck rubbed her eyes. "Dad's eyes are giving him trouble. He's had a marathon headache ever since this thing began. And last night after everybody had left, he complained that the documents he was reading kept growing blurry."

A gruff-looking man walked by with a gruff-looking Schnauzer on a leash.

"Ever notice how much people resemble their pets?" whispered Stan.

"Exactly what I was thinking." I finished the cocoa and handed the cup back to her. "Felicity Licht likes birds because she's as dry as a stick and so plain. Parrots possess the splendor she's lacking."

"I can't wait to see her." Stanwyck clapped her mittened hands together.

I hated to see Stanwyck pinning so much hope on Felicity. It's her way to take a few drops of reality and expand them into a full-scale drama. This time it was partially my fault, carrying on about the dreary woman as if she were a mysteri-

65

ous spy in a fog-bound thirties movie. "What about Noah?" I asked to get the subject back to safer ground.

Stanwyck looked at me questioningly, her head to one side like a cartoon bird. "Oh, Noah! Right! He's cruising the boards, pretending to have a brand-new 800-number phreak that he wants to try in England or France or South America." She crumpled up the doughnut wrappings into the paper bag and blotted her sticky fingers against the side of the building.

"What does he hope to find out? We already know the codes they used."

"But we have to uncover who used the codes! You know phreakers can't resist bragging about their latest crack. And this one is a cosmic phreak, let's face it. Thousands of dollars in one month for a few calls to Brazil. It's an awesome phreak, one to be proud of."

"Stanwyck, this cosmic phreak is the main nail hanging your father."

"Thanks for reminding me. For thirty seconds I forgot why we were camped out here waiting for the Birdwoman to drop the evidence into our laps."

"Have you considered the possibility that she's a blind alley? Like Terrapin Circle itself." I gestured at the high gates across the street from the doorway in which we were huddled. "They're still padlocked."

"Locking themselves in or us out? Either way, it's probably illegal," Stanwyck said. "It's a public thoroughfare."

"Interesting how spotless they keep it. No graffiti and no garbage cans. I wonder what they do with their garbage."

"Maybe they keep it inside their houses until it decomposes." Stanwyck dipped a couple of marshmallows into the cocoa. "It's only eight thirty. Rats! I can't wait to see this Felicity bird."

"Mornin', detectives," said an amused male voice. "Lovely day for catching bird smugglers."

It was Ray Brown in his dark three-piece suit and raincoat.

"Don't you know how to relax?" exclaimed Stanwyck. "You must have at least seen pictures of guys wearing jeans and boots and hanging out."

"I'm working, lady. Remember what your father said yesterday. He's paying the firm's hefty legal rates. With three of us by the hour, we're talking big bucks. Have to sell a lot of mattresses to pay our fees."

"You're disgusting," said Stanwyck.

He did not take offense. His face crinkled into a broad grin, and he patted Stan's shoulder. "It's my job to make sure Mr. Baum gets his money's worth. We've got solid evidence about Caracas that Gadamer worked through yesterday. That Lou is a real jewel. He never gives up—keeps pulling at the facts, so patiently until finally they unravel. Unlike that new guy—what's his name, Tom—who is supposed to be working on the calls to Rio."

"And what are you doing? Supervising?"

"In a matter of speaking, Miss Baum. I drew the short straw on this case. I'm watching you and Watson. Now please, over here." He pointed to each of us in turn.

"Get lost!" I jumped to my feet. "We didn't ask for a baby-sitter." I longed to spatter mud onto his gleaming wing-tip shoes and his perfectly pressed trenchcoat. But it hadn't rained in days. The gutters were bone dry.

"Client's request. Mr. Baum has figured out that you two are playing detective, and he wants to make sure you don't become a bigger headache to him than the feds."

"Keep away from us, Ray Brown!" I felt ludicrous as I flailed the air.

He flashed that ever-patient grin. "If it's Sunday, this must be a stakeout. There is a suspect?"

What was the use? There's no dignity in outrage. "We might as well tell him, Stanwyck. He's got a real unmovable set to his shoulders. We're not going to be able to shake him easily."

"About an hour from now, we're going to meet Felicity Licht, and you cannot come with us. She's a very bizarre person who lives in Terrapin Circle in that house with the dark green shutters. She has an aviary where she keeps exotic parrots, and she just may be the smugglers' connection. But she's not the type to lead guided tours of her house, so you'll have to wait on this side of the street. At the hourly rate, of course."

His manner changed abruptly. "You've actually found an aviary this close to the loft? Excellent work! That could explain the bags of bird feathers."

Stanwyck and I exchanged puzzled looks. Ray Brown got out a pad and uncapped a fountain pen. "Felicity Licht, right? I'll get a couple of paralegals to pull background on her while you two are inside the house. Now, be sure to check for garbage cans near the aviary. Two, see where she keeps the parrot food. Naturally one of you must keep a careful count of the number of birds. Three, try to remember the patterns of some of them so we can get a bird expert to identify what species she's got. If they can be traced to Brazil and Venezuela, we are in a much better position than I thought possible while I was shaving this morning."

I gave him a sidelong glance. "Thanks to teenage investigators?"

"Okay, I apologize for my patronizing attitude. You may have uncovered something. Now, don't let her get suspicious. One of you ask her the questions, and the other try to memorize the color patterns."

"We'll do better than that," I told him. "We'll take the curator of birds from the Museum of Natural History to identify the birds."

"I'm serious." Ray Brown frowned. "Don't treat this lightly."

"She's serious, too! We're very thorough. We'd never research an aviary without a first-class expert along. Lucky for Daddy, we don't have to pay Dr. Winston Flyte, curator of birds, by the hour. He's interested in justice."

"Just like Superman. Now, what about going around the corner for some breakfast? My treat."

"Sounds great," I said quickly.

"Can't leave the stakeout," Stanwyck reminded me.

"Sure we can. We're going to get all the information we need inside her house."

"Suppose she dumps evidence because we're coming?"

"Why don't you wait here, and Watson and I will have breakfast?" suggested Ray Brown. I flashed Stanwyck my most secret signal, and mercifully she got it.

"Excellent suggestion. Jess has been working almost non-stop since Dad's arrest. She can fill you in on our discoveries."

"Then it's settled. We won't be gone long, Stanwyck." Ray

Brown put his note pad and pen into his coat pocket. "That place with the palm trees in the window, over toward West Broadway. Is that okay with you?"

"Sounds fine," I said, winking to Stan as we headed away from Terrapin Circle.

"Lots of hot coffee." He sighed. "This is going to be a long week. I have to get back to the Coast next week for the beginning of some high-level merger negotiations. So we'd better box these birds in the next couple of days." He guided me toward the restaurant. "Eggs and bacon? Maybe a cheese omelet?"

I shuddered. "Not eggs. They're bird coffins."

"You're not letting this parrot business get to you, old girl," he said. Suddenly we were talking as if we'd known each other for years. If it hadn't been Mr. Baum in such trouble, I could have forgotten about parrots for the rest of the day.

When Dr. Flyte removed his spectacles, his eyes were almost perfectly round—like a bird's. He rubbed his gloved hands together nervously. "Now, girls, it would be better if you stuck to the story about buying your mother a parrot. An African Gray would be appropriate. She's not good with people, dear Felicity. The African Gray is a charmer, a real social bird." When he was outside his laboratory, he stammered nervously. "Perhaps you could be doing a report for school." He looked unconvinced at his own suggestion.

"We shoot from the hip. The stakes are too high," Stanwyck told him. When I had returned to our outpost across from Terrapin Circle, I saw that Stanwyck had decorated herself suitably for mingling with exotic birds. She had braided her hair and secured the braid on top of her head. She had tucked the pile of hair inside a red and blue ski cap. She looked almost crested. With a bright green scarf and gold knit gloves, she was very birdy. As usual, I felt dull and predictable, but I hoped I was the sort of person Felicity would feel comfortable with. She might be tempted to tame Stanwyck and feed her seeds from the palm of her hand.

We made an odd threesome, pushing against the heavy gates of the Circle. "Look! The gates are padlocked," said Dr. Flyte. "How shall we get inside?"

A burly man came to the door of the first house. "We're not open to tourists," he shouted through a partially open door. "Try Bleecker Street."

My heart pounded with excitement. "We're here to visit Felicity Licht, your neighbor," I called to him. The door opened a bit wider, and he checked us out. Before he could make up his mind, the door of the second house opened. Felicity, with her head thrust out in front of her, inched stiff-legged down her steps, never looking up from the ground. She moved slowly but deliberately. A large key on a thick rope dangled from her wrist. Her shoulders were rolled forward and hunched up toward her ears. Her arms were crossed in front of her, as if protecting a secret hidden deep within herself. She unlocked the gate with two quick efficient thrusts of the key but still didn't raise her head.

As the heavy gate swung open, she stood aside. "Hello, Dr. Flyte," she said in a voice as soft as air. She said nothing to Stanwyck and me. The fingers of both hands curled under as if she were clutching an invisible perch. Although she was

71

several inches taller than either of us, I felt enormous beside her. I stepped back, uncomfortable next to her, fearing I would knock her over with one strong breath.

As we followed Felicity and Dr. Flyte up the stairs into her house, Stanwyck whispered to me, "She's like something out of a fairy tale. Look at her skin! A dark princess who's been dead or asleep for a hundred years."

I signaled to Stanwyck to be quiet, but I had the same eerie feeling myself. I walked stiff-legged, too; I sensed that we were doomed children being led toward a poisoned apple prepared especially for us. Felicity draped her raincoat over the banister of a steep, carpeted stairway. She did not offer to take our coats.

There were several space heaters in the hallway of the second floor. "Having problems with drafts," she said, her voice barely audible. "Several budgies refusing food, going light," she said.

"French molt?" asked Dr. Flyte. His own voice had shrunk almost to a whisper to match hers.

Noiselessly, she led us up another flight of stairs and paused in front of a glass-paneled door. Stanwyck and I had become invisible.

"No worry of shock in the parrots. They're stronger than mahogany."

"You've hand-raised most of the birds in this aviary, haven't you?"

She seemed incapable of answering direct questions.

"The girls want to know the names of some aviculturists who might help them locate Brazilian birds. Has there been a large quantity of conures or parrots imported recently?"

"These are the parrot aviaries," she said, as if he hadn't spoken. "The birds who live on this floor don't require as much flight space as the larger parakeets." When she spoke, her facial expression did not change; her eyes stayed downcast. Her body remained still. "They can see the birds through the glass," she said. Soundlessly, she let herself into the aviary.

"She keeps the macaws and cockatoos upstairs. They require wider areas, although not so much flight space." Drawn by the sounds of the birds clattering within, Dr. Flyte peered into the aviary. Felicity nodded to him, and he sighed happily as he entered the room full of birds.

"She makes my flesh creep," muttered Stanwyck. "She's probably got green blood, the color of that bird fluttering near Dr. Flyte." We pressed against the glass and looked into an utterly different world, as unlike ours as the one inside a sugar-coated Easter egg.

A brilliant blue bird with copper wings lit on Felicity's shoulder. At the touch of the bird's curled toes, Felicity became transformed. She stood up straight; her neck became long and straight. Her eyes were raised to the high perches in the aviary. We could hear her making sounds to the birds; her voice was strong and resonant. A scarlet bird with an enormous hooked beak landed on her outstretched arm and curled its head upside down flirtatiously. She stroked its head; her own eyes were half closed. It rubbed his beak against the palm of her hand.

"Look at those long tail feathers!" whispered Stanwyck, pointing to a pair of green and yellow birds sharing a perch near the door. "To live with a bird as beautiful as that. Look!

It's got pink around its neck, like a collar. How could anyone hurt such a creature?"

I looked at Stanwyck to see if she was joking. But she seemed completely spellbound by the birds within the aviary.

Dr. Flyte did not follow Felicity into the larger central aviary. When she unlocked the front cage, a large lavender and green bird with yellow markings on its head flew to the perch nearest her.

Puckering her lips, she called "*Cherreep ch-ch-ch-cherreep*" as her head circled slowly. She cupped her hands, and the bird flew into the cradle she'd made. She blew lightly on the bird's wings until the bird preened; its feathers puffed out. Felicity continued to make sounds I'd never heard. The other birds grew restless, flying to different perches, imitating her voice—or was she imitating theirs?

She reached into her pocket and offered the bird some seeds. The bird teased her, flying backward toward the perch. Then, at the last minute, it swerved and landed on a perch directly above Felicity's head. She lifted up her long arms: they became branches. The bird stretched its neck and took the seeds from her outstretched hands, cracking the shells with its beak.

A coral and orange bird fluttered around Felicity's head and landed on her shoulder. "*Corra, recorra,*" the bird called, her wing beating against Felicity's cheek. She turned her head and poked her beak deep within Felicity's ear. Felicity remained still until the bird quieted herself, rubbing herself against the woman's neck.

"I feel like we shouldn't be watching," I whispered to

Stanwyck. "As if she were naked and we were peeping toms."

"She's awesome. I've never seen anyone cross species lines like that. In that aviary she is bird." Stanwyck turned to me, her face pink with excitement. "We've suspected the wrong person. She isn't a smuggler. She isn't evil."

I shivered. "Don't be fooled by these dazzling birds. I have a feeling that if one of us licked her face, we'd be poisoned."

Chapter Six

Mr. Baum was lying down with a cold cloth on his head because his eyes were burning. He had a foul toothache that had turned into a raging headache. He held a sofa cushion to his left cheek and moved restlessly on the couch. The legal team were tiptoeing around, discussing things in whispers, doing their best to let the poor man suffer in peace. Thomas offered to call the dentist, but Mr. Baum swore under his breath. Apparently he and Dr. Thaddeus had had a major fight over a root canal last year, and he'd never give the guy the satisfaction.

Mrs. Baum was lying down with a warm cloth over her face because tension had frozen her sinuses. Her entire face ached. It was certainly no ordinary weekday, with Mr. Baum at home and lawyers swarming all over the loft. We had one more week of winter recess, and days were mushed together.

It was afternoon, but we'd picked the refrigerator clean before eleven that morning. Ray had sent Lou Gadamer and Thomas out for pizza; he seemed to be the one in charge. Lou was the most amiable of the three. A quiet man, he did the lion's share of the work. Ray Brown was like my history teacher, Mr. Scarborough. He delegated mountains of work, then looked surprised when people groaned that there was no way to get through that much in a week's time.

Stanwyck was at her computer, cruising the boards. While we were still eating breakfast, Noah had arrived with his portable computer. Now he was sitting beside Stanwyck, efficient as ever, his eyes squinted to the messages filling up his screen. He and Stanwyck were determined to find the phreakers who had participated in the Brazil phone crack before Mr. Sheldon met with the prosecutors on Wednesday morning.

"Somebody's got to let us in on the foreign 800 game. I haven't found a single board where it's discussed." Noah talked as he typed, systematically checking BBS by area code.

"There don't seem to be any new code words—of course. I'm looking for coffee beans and sombreros—"

"And Juan Valdez operating a major phone crack?" I asked.

"It's our only major lead. There has to be a phreaker who's running a crack threading Brazilian and Venezuelan calls through Dad's number. They pound the 800 number through the Latin American connection—"

I was losing patience. "I know how they do it, Stanwyck. But you haven't produced any proof that anyone actually is doing it. Ray Brown says we have to find one actual phreak from Brazil. It doesn't have to be hooked into your father's number, just enough for reasonable doubt."

"Thanks, Jess. We might not have figured that out." Stanwyck bent her head to the keyboard, like Schroeder

77

playing a cartoon piano. It seemed counterproductive to point out to Stan that I was not to blame for her father's troubles. When it was all over, she'd apologize without my having to demand it.

I went into the living room, wondering how long it would be before Mr. Baum was the Mattress King again. "I have no one to play with," I said to Ray Brown.

"There's plenty of work to do. All Lou was able to turn up on that Felicity Licht is that she has full title to the house; it has no mortgage; apparently she inherited it from her father. We're running a credit check on her, but so far we haven't turned up anything significant. I'd like you to write up a memo on what you saw yesterday in that woman's house."

"I don't need to write it down. I'll never forget that place. You know, some of those birds were really good talkers. There was one macaw who spoke in sharp clear tones, like a human. She must have spent months teaching him."

"Don't tell me; write it down. Lawyers write memos after every client conversation. Believe me, three months from now you won't remember what your Parrot Woman was wearing, much less what her birds sounded like. You'll forget if the lights were on in the stairway; how many birds were in the aviary; what kind of wire fences enclosed the cages. Details, my dear Watson. Please write down all the details for me."

I looked at him silently. It was barely twenty-four hours later, and already I couldn't remember what Felicity had been wearing except for the black raincoat. There must have been lights in the stairway; after all, we could see our way up to the third floor. Or was it the fourth?

Reluctantly, I reached for a yellow legal pad and began to write down every detail: "All the hallways were carpeted in a pale color; maybe gray. There were space heaters on the second floor. Some of her birds seemed to be sick, but I didn't catch that conversation. There were no sounds in the house, except that the birds were screaming and talking when we were standing directly outside the aviary. But you couldn't hear the birds as you were going up the stairs. If you hadn't known there were aviaries in the house, you'd never have guessed from standing on the first floor."

Noah came to the door of the living area. "Stanwyck wants you inside," he said to me. He seemed uncomfortable with Ray Brown. Noah's shyness had improved since the days when his only friends were anonymous BBS users. But he had a way to go before he'd be a talk-show host. With people he didn't know, like Ray Brown, he stared at the ground when he spoke, his sentences shorn of anything other than the absolutely essential.

"Have you all found any promising leads?" asked Ray Brown.

Noah shook his head.

"I'll finish this list later," I assured Ray. "The talking macaw was blue and gold with a hooked black beak. Ugly as a weapon."

Stanwyck came in and waved a print-out at me. "Stop gossiping about the birds! We're on to something *major*. A sysop in Oklahoma who operates the Volume Board sent me this note."

Standing in front of Ray Brown, she began to read: " 'We've been phreaking 800 numbers connected to one of the TV record clubs for about six weeks. And we've got two projects hanging on the boards for volume calls to Puerto Rico. If you want to join, send us your handle, the Brazilian phone crack you mentioned, and then if it all checks out, we'll download our codes to you in hex. To prevent them falling into the wrong hands.' "

Noah pulled Stanwyck's keyboard onto his lap and began typing rapidly: "*I'm Mister Rogers, sysop of the Head Board. We can orchestrate together, Volume Board. You don't have to check* me *out. Send sysop info.*" His fingers slammed the keys in anger. "Coding in hex. Can't I tell him who you are, Stanwyck?"

"I feel like we're falling backward in a time machine, Stan," I objected. "We promised the police and our parents that we'd never get involved with these bulletin boards again. We're on probation, in case you've forgotten. I don't want to graduate from reform school."

"Be careful—as a lawyer, I'm an officer of the court." Ray Brown was standing in the doorway, snickering at our discomfort. "But I'm off duty till the pizza gets here."

"You work for my father. My room is off limits to your investigation," snapped Stanwyck. "I won't poke around in your legal business. You leave the phreaker work to me. I'm the Perry Mason of phreakers."

"Watson's right, Stanwyck." Ray Brown's face grew serious. "There are federal agents crawling all over this place. They've probably got a tap on your phone. They could very well be sitting in an unmarked van a block from here, spilling data siphoned from your modem hookup. They can wire into your lines and pick up everything you download, as well as what you're sending out over the phone lines. Use some sense."

Noah's shoulders slumped. "I bet they have surveillance procedures we haven't thought of."

"Then we'll take the computer and the modem to somebody's else's house."

Ray Brown looked at her admiringly. "Obstacles don't hold you in one place long. Flexibility is the key to success." He put his arm around Stanwyck. "This print-out about the Puerto Rico connection could be the key to something. We'd have to find out how to identify the person for the DA to accept it as evidence. Otherwise, you kids could've typed it up yourselves."

"Stanwyck's a gymnast on the keyboard," I told him.

"Remember what Sheldon told us. If you can get print-outs that prove these volume phone phreaks are widespread, we'll be able to cast doubt on their major piece of evidence."

"We've shown that the feathers could have come from Felicity's aviary," I said with pride. "That's one place I don't want to go back to."

Stanwyck looked at me angrily. "She's not involved in this smuggling racket. Anyone who could communicate so lovingly with those birds—I think the Hyacinth Macaw is her favorite. Remember how it lay on her chest while she stroked its head?"

"It's her communication with people that's under scrutiny," Ray Brown reminded Stanwyck. "Be careful about getting too involved, Stan. This may not turn out the way you'd like it to."

"We couldn't actually match any feathers to any of her

birds. Let's not drum up evidence merely to throw suspicion off my father."

"Okay, protect your Parrot Woman, Stanwyck. All that's important to me is that we've significantly weakened the prosecutor's case. Of course, we'll need to produce more hard evidence before we can insist on a public apology, which is the only thing that will restore Mr. Baum's standing in the community."

"Well spoken, counselor," said Stanwyck. Her attention was already back on the message coming across her screen. She seemed willing to drop the subject of the Parrot Woman, which was fine with me.

Apparently satisfied that we would not bring the feds to the loft to make another series of arrests, Ray Brown went back to the living room.

"Start packing up the disks, Noah. As soon as this guy terminates with me, we'll move on uptown," Stanwyck said firmly. "The sooner we hang these phreakers, the sooner we can leave the poor Parrot Woman in peace with her birds."

"We're not setting up shop at my house," I said quickly. "My mother would call the cops herself."

Stanwyck looked questioningly at Noah. "Impossible," he said. "Father's turned over the house to visiting scholars from Jerusalem. They fill up every inch of the place. Sleeping on mattresses, reading Torah late into the night, eating special kosher food in plastic bowls brought in by Mrs. Arnstein downstairs."

"Sounds like a day at the beach," muttered Stanwyck. "What about the Beak? No one would suspect him!"

"His mom is a vulture. She feeds off punishments."

"Jess will charm her." Stanwyck smiled and continued to talk as she downloaded the remaining info on disk. "Jess is awesome at bending adults to her will."

"Not vultures," I insisted. "Let's leave the Beak in peace. He delivered Dr. Flyte to us. He's more than earned a day of peace."

"And my dad?" demanded Stanwyck. "What's he earned?"

"Let's call the Beak," I said, gathering the print-outs, which were strewn all over the room. "Operation Caracas continues."

"In case she answers, his mom calls him Simon," said Noah, handing the phone to Stanwyck.

"May I speak with Simon, please? This is Stanwyck Baum," purred Stanwyck. "I see. Well, this is very important. Could I speak to him for a moment?"

She hung up the phone. "Simon is being punished. He may not speak to his friends for three days."

"No wonder he's offended by cages," I said.

"Pizza's here!" called Ray Brown.

"Told you she was a vulture."

"Guess it's my house," I said, picking up the modem. "My mom may not be pleased, but she won't rip off our wings."

Lou was complaining to Ray Brown, slapping the kitchen counter to emphasize his points. The pressure was getting to him. Melodrama seeped out around him. I thought of the stillness of Dr. Flyte and Felicity Licht. She communicated with her birds without a sound. While Stanwyck and I watched from the hallway behind the glass doors, a Double-Crested Cockatoo had flown to Felicity's shoulder and had gently picked roasted pumpkin seeds from between her lips.

I'd never seen such intimacy between a human being and an animal.

"He hasn't been pulling his weight. I don't know why Sheldon wanted him on board. Now he's gone off somewhere—"

"Who's he talking about?" I whispered to Stanwyck.

"Thomas has apparently flown our merry little coop."

"He didn't say where he was going?" asked Ray Brown.

"Said he had some personal errands."

"We've been working around the clock. He's entitled to a few hours off," Ray pointed out.

"While we were going through the past year's transactions with the client's U.S. and Canadian suppliers of feathers and down this morning, Thomas did nothing except talk about dentists with Mr. Baum." Lou flung himself down onto the couch. He took the beer can that Stanwyck offered him. "Did he get your father to go to the dentist?"

"Thomas isn't going to get Dad to any dentist. Dad's not a big fan of Dr. Thaddeus. He hasn't been there since that root canal blew his jaw up to the size of a watermelon." Stanwyck snatched up a piece of pizza. "The dentist told me Dad was one of his most challenging patients. He cancels so many appointments that Dr. Thaddeus never writes him in the book anymore. He works Dad in if he shows up. Of course, if I miss even one miserable drilling session, I'm dead in the water. Talk about unequal laws!"

"You'd be a great litigator, Stanwyck. I'd love to see you working a jury." Lou chuckled and pulled pieces of sausage off the slices remaining in the pizza box. "As long as we were on the same side, of course."

"We going?" Noah asked me in a whisper. He had packed the modem and his computer into a shopping bag. He handed me a box of disks.

"Let's see if you can convince my mom that we're not hooking up a modem and a computer in her house when that is clearly what we're doing."

Filled with confidence, Stanwyck wrapped a scarf around Noah's neck. "Keep warm. We'll need your keyboarding magic when we get uptown." She altered her voice, injecting its "around adults" tone: "You see, Mrs. Graham, we have this special project for our computing class at school. And since everything is in such chaos at the loft, we needed a quiet place to work. We shouldn't leave our computations till the last moment, so even though it's winter break, we thought we should work all day."

"My mom's not that gullible," I warned her.

My mom was that gullible. She praised us for working during vacation. She praised us for using computers the way they were meant to be used. She didn't question us about the status of the case or about Mr. Baum. I gave her a quick kiss. "You're turning into a model parent," I said.

"It's the least I can do," she said modestly. "If involving herself in a school project can keep poor Stanwyck's mind off her father's troubles, so much the better."

"They've got flocks of lawyers flying around the loft," I offered. "They think they can prove that all the feathers came from suppliers Mr. Baum has used for more than ten years. And the bit about payoffs from the smuggling—well, there are no big sums of money deposited in any of his accounts. The lawyers seem quite hopeful," I added, because it seemed like the proper thing to say. Ray Brown had looked far from hopeful as he'd helped us load our equipment into a cab. "If you don't turn up any BBS phone cracks to or from Latin America by six o'clock, call me, and we'll put our computer mavens on it. We don't have time to waste, kids."

Stanwyck was lying on my bed. "I don't want to get a reputation as a worm. How can we turn phreakers in to the feds?"

"How can you let your father take the fall?" I asked.

"If only there were some way to clear Daddy's name without pulling the plug on some major phreak."

"I've got this guy from Worcester who participated in a volume phreak for a month, ordering little thimbles with pictures of the Presidents' wives on them. The computer was set to break the phone connection as soon as the 800 number connected. So the calls were charged to the thimble company, but the caller wasn't stuck with the thimbles. Listen to this—they got more than three thousand calls in one month. What a phreak!" Noah looked flushed. *"I wouldn't mind phreaking in on a crack like that,"* he typed hastily.

"We're running one from Guatemala," the guy typed back. *"We hook into a random number, then call Guatemala using the standard sequence, loop into 800, and they trace the crack back to the number we're linked to. We are totally safe from detection. It's a double bucky shanghai crack. We can run up charges twice as heavy on the 800 line."*

"Stanwyck, this is hot!" said Noah. "You'd better watch this develop." He typed rapidly, *"Who's the sysop? Mr. Rogers wants in."*

86

For several hours we followed every lead, calling each person suggested by each sysop we contacted. I worked the phone while Noah and Stanwyck called over the modem using their computers. It seemed as if everyone had heard of volume phone phreaks, although not everyone was into them. Too many kids had been trapped by the feds for participating in major phreaks. Many veteran phreakers were now more cautious than they had been a year earlier.

It was almost four o'clock when I wandered into the living room. Mother was reading the afternoon paper. "Nothing about the case," she said, a note of disappointment in her voice. "Nothing on the morning news, either."

"Mom, this is a noncase. The feds are going to end up with egg on their faces. Mr. Baum is totally innocent. Anyway, there's nothing new to report."

"I'm surprised one of those Save the Birds groups isn't picketing his factory. Mattresses stuffed with parrot feathers—it even gives me the creeps, and I've known Mel Baum since Stanwyck started school with you in the fourth grade."

I laughed until my sides ached. "Mom, he's not accused of using parrot feathers in his mattresses. He's accused of smuggling live birds for profit," I explained through fits of laughter.

"Jess! Come quickly!" shouted Stanwyck.

She and Noah were hugging each other. "You can be the first to see our evidence, Ms. Graham," said Stanwyck, reaching for the hairbrush on my bureau. Whenever she gets very excited, Stanwyck combs her hair to steady her nerves. "Read it on the screen. We'll print out the disk as soon as we get downtown."

Noah read aloud the words on the screen. " 'Call Rambo's

Fingerman in Connecticut. He's got the major code cracks for the Guatemala gig. It's a sequence of numbers that runs for three days, then changes for two days, then back to the original for three days. It should be hard to trace because each phreaker will only program a week of cracked code. This guy was the control behind one in Peru, I think it was. Where all the coffee comes from.' " Noah turned to Stanwyck, who was bent over. The tips of her hair almost touched the ground, and she was brushing as if pieces of evidence were buried in her hair.

She stood upright; her hair fanned out around her. "I can't wait to see the look on Ray Brown's face."

"Bet your mom's sinus headache will vanish," I said. "It's all over. We won the case!"

"Get serious, Jess. I'm no lawyer, but this isn't real hard evidence. It merely casts a doubt on their case. Remember what old Ray told us. It's not hard evidence; it merely proves that these phone cracks are commonplace."

My mother was having trouble holding on to her model parent role. "You're to sleep here tonight, Jess. They have enough going on at the Baums' without you as a permanent guest. Finish this project tomorrow. You are to be home by ten o'clock."

"I promise, Mom. I'll be back in a couple hours. After I help Stanwyck home with all her gear. There's no need for me to stay downtown tonight. Mr. Baum's troubles are about to fly away as suddenly as they came."

"Light as a feather," added Stanwyck.

Noah hugged the bag with his computer and smiled shyly at Mom as the elevator doors closed.

*   *   *

We waited with Noah till his subway train came, and then we crossed the platform and got on the train going downtown. When we got to the loft, Mrs. Baum was stirring a large pot of soup. "Everyone's gone," she said, staring into the pot.

"Drowned in the soup?" asked Stanwyck, kissing her mother's cheek.

"I'm in no mood for jokes. At least that sweet boy Thomas got your father to go to the dentist. Some special pain specialist he'd read about agreed to see Mel immediately. Guarantees to work without pain. I don't know how Thomas did it. Mel must be in excruciating pain." She put the wooden spoon on the counter. "When will this nightmare end?"

"In about an hour," said Stanwyck calmly. "As soon as we print out this message. Where's Ray Brown?"

"He went home. He can't stay here around the clock."

"At his hourly rate, he'd love to stay here all the time," Stanwyck said. "But we've found the key, the missing link, the magic that will free Daddy, and all thanks to me and Jess."

"Oh, darling, if only that were true!" She stirred the soup one more time and covered the pot.

"It may be true," I said while Stanwyck was in her room printing out the message. In most of our dealings with parents, I'm the voice of reason who gives stability to Stanwyck's bubbles. "We have proof that phreakers have been working volume phone cracks in Peru and Guatemala and in some country where they grow coffee." I had lowered my voice in imitation of Stanwyck's tone of heavy drama. It came out like a growl, causing Mrs. Baum to frown.

"All this dashing about and standing outside in the cold—you're coming down with something, Jess. And your mother will be right to hold me responsible."

"Mom, will you listen? We've found evidence!" shouted Stanwyck, returning with the computer print-out.

"What evidence?" Mr. Baum, followed by Thomas, entered the loft. "I can't read anything for a while, Stanwyck. That dentist was a marvel. Shot me full of pain-killers. He shined lights and mirrors into my eyes. I must have been in that chair an hour, and yet it seemed like only a few minutes. That's how good he is. Can't feel that tooth at all."

Thomas examined the print-out. "Looks convincing. I'll be glad to take it downtown. Mr. Sheldon is meeting with us tonight at ten."

"At the hourly rate," said Stanwyck.

"That's enough!" her father answered severely. "These boys have saved my hide. And I'll always be grateful."

"Dad," said Stanwyck, tears in her eyes, "*we* got this evidence, Jess and Noah and I, not your hotshot lawyers! C'mon, Jess, let's go get something to eat. Away from here." She grabbed her coat and mine. Without pausing to find our gloves and scarves, we left the loft.

"I'm sick of him never crediting me with anything." Stanwyck slammed the front door of the building.

I glanced at Terrapin Circle as we walked toward Broadway, but it was dark. There were no lights visible in Felicity's house. She probably keeps bird hours, I thought, unwilling to share the joke with Stanwyck, whose face was still angry.

"Look down there, Jess."

"I don't see anything."

"Open your eyes! It looks like someone's trying to hotwire that car." Sure enough, there was a figure bent over the rear of a car. "There's smoke coming out of the exhaust pipe. The motor is running."

"He's trying to steal the car," said Stanwyck, quickening her pace.

As we ran toward the fellow, we saw that the left front door of the car was open. There were several small brown bags near him on the sidewalk. We hid in a doorway about ten yards from him, clutching each other. "Is there a phone where we can call the cops?" I whispered to Stanwyck. She shrugged and put her fingers to her lips.

The man had a soft-brimmed hat pulled down over his head. He went to the front seat and removed a package. Without getting into the car, he stepped on the accelerator and revved the engine a few times. Then, holding the package under his coat, he hurried toward the back of the car, his head tucked down into his chest.

When he got to the rear of the car, he placed the opening of the brown bag over the exhaust pipe of the car. He remained crouched over the bag for several moments. Then we heard a low moan as if he were in pain.

Stanwyck clutched my hand, and we crept toward him, our hearts pounding. My foot hit a stone, causing me to stumble. The man looked up.

It was Felicity Licht. Her face was wet with tears.

Stanwyck knelt beside her. "What's the matter?"

"Birds in terminal shock. It's the kindest way." She put the brown bag onto the sidewalk next to the others. Stanwyck looked inside the bag and screamed, "You've been killing the birds!"

She began hitting Felicity on the chest and arms, raining blows wherever she could. I tried to stop her, but Stanwyck pushed me backward, sending me sprawling on the sidewalk.

Felicity slumped onto the ground, accepting Stanwyck's blows. After several minutes she reached up and pinned Stanwyck's arms to her sides. "Hush, hush," she said, her voice whooshing like the wings of the birds in her aviary. She stroked Stanwyck's hair, murmuring softly to her.

My eyes went to the plump bags on the sidewalk, and I shuddered. With no one to witness her act, she'd been gassing the birds as calmly as she'd fed them the day before.

"Come back to the house. We'll feed the chicks. You'll understand the balance," she whispered, her arm around Stanwyck's trembling shoulders.

To my surprise, Stanwyck rested her head against Felicity's chest. "The birds," she said. "Take me with you and show me the birds."

I grabbed Stanwyck's arm. "Don't be crazy! We're going out for supper."

Stanwyck looked at me coldly. "Go home, Jess. I'll talk to you tomorrow." She looked up at Felicity, searching her face for the feeling of birds.

Chapter Seven

As soon as I'd bolted some cereal under the watchful eye of my mother the next morning, I hurried to the loft to hear what had happened at the aviary. I'd waited up till after midnight, assuming Stan would call me after she left Felicity's bird heaven, but there had been no call. That could mean Stan had swallowed another dose of birdiness and was going to be flighty.

Mrs. Baum was wandering around the loft, straightening cushions and looking blanker than usual. "This business with Mel has finally got to the poor child," Mrs. Baum told me. "She won't talk to anyone. She won't eat—not even corn muffins and jam. She won't come out of her room. Well, the lawyers say it should all be over soon. Thank the Lord, the government seems willing to drop the case now."

"That is the best news," I said, forcing myself to sound cheerful. Clearly that old witch had put one of her parrot spells on Stan.

"Dear David Sheldon has been negotiating with them all morning."

Stanwyck was unwilling to talk even to me. As I sat on her bed and pointed out that we'd actually provided the evidence to clear her father—something to be proud of—she stared out the window, unblinking. She was still in her nightgown. Her hair had not been freshly braided; it was straggling and frizzled. "Want me to comb your hair?"

She looked at me, puzzled. "Inside my head is like her aviary. Remember how it sounded? There's so much cheeping, you can't hear one particular bird? Well, I can't hear one clear voice, even my own. Felicity knew that without my ever telling her. Sitting in her kitchen drinking tea, she tidied up the inside of my head without saying anything. Being in her presence unravels all the knots in my head. Do you understand, Jess?"

I was vastly uncomfortable, looking at Stanwyck's tense expression. I hadn't had a clue that there had been this roaring inside her. If only I'd sensed that she had been hearing a cacophany of birds. I'd always assumed that Stan's thoughts were much the same as my own. Of course, my father had never been accused of a major crime. "Let's forget Felicity. As long as they're dropping the case against your father, we don't have to turn her in to the feds if you don't want to. I suppose it's not a crime to gas your own birds."

Stanwyck closed her eyes. "Don't ever say that again," she said in an ominously quiet tone. "We'll never reveal what we saw on Spring Street."

Having witnessed Stanwyck slide into hysterics the night before, I didn't need any encouragement to keep the entire incident quiet. I needed time to forget those brown bags, so like school lunch bags. But in spite of my revulsion, I knew that gassing birds wasn't the same as smuggling them. The Parrot Woman might be utterly loony tunes, but she wasn't a criminal. It seemed almost impossible that the radiant woman who'd crooned to her parrots was the same as the one holding bags to the exhaust pipe of an idling car. I felt helpless because Stanwyck seemed to care so much.

"Guess I'll go home."

"Watching her with the birds, I almost believed she could fly."

"Stan, you're allowing yourself to flip out!" I said angrily. "You know she can't fly. She's just an eccentric who raises birds in her house. You're tricking yourself into this birdiness. Don't make it more than it is."

She looked at me with tears in her eyes. "For a moment, while we were watching through the glass, I wished I was one of those birds. I wished I could live in that aviary and be warmed under her hands and be fed by her and snuggle with those other parrots and feel my wings grow stronger until I could fly to the high perch, too."

It's a mood, I assured myself. Stanwyck can talk herself into anything. "Call me when you pull out of this, and we'll try to salvage what's left of vacation." I tried to hug her, but she held her body stiffly. "I'm glad your dad is going to be cleared. That's the important thing."

Riding home on the bus, I tried to think of other times when she'd taken flight to a corner of her mind where I couldn't follow. She does get over these things, I reminded myself. In less than two days she'd dropped the phreaking of computer games after doing nothing else for months. This

95

bird business would be shed as easily as the pile of molted feathers that the ecology guy had dumped in front of the loft. As my mother says about ten times a day, whatever is bothering you now will seem very unimportant next month. Growing up is only a matter of time.

"Hi there, Watson. Thought you'd like to witness the conclusion to your first major case." Ray Brown's voice sounded more formal on the phone than in person. "Tomorrow morning at the Federal Building at eleven o'clock. Seventeenth floor. A press conference and a public apology to our client, Mel Baum. By noon, he'll be able to go back to being Mattress King."

I was surprised that Stanwyck hadn't called to tell me the news. "Who else will be there?"

"It's not a party. Just the press and the family and probably some very embarrassed agents. You'll recognize them easily. They'll be the ones with egg on their faces."

"Could I invite Noah? He helped us crack the phreaker code. In case the feds want to interview the teenage investigators."

"Sure, bring him along. But it's not going to be an all-day affair. I imagine the whole apology will take about ten minutes. They won't be anxious to stretch this thing out. If the feds get lucky and there's a major train derailment or a highway flooding or a nine-car pileup, it won't even make the evening news."

"That won't happen." I laughed. "By the way, we have some unfinished business. Remember, Ray, I like my steak rare."

"It's not over till it's over." He laughed. "I still have time to weasel out of our bet."

"I'll hire a state-of-the-art lawyer to make you pay up. Maybe Thomas."

"He hasn't been around the past couple days. Nobody told him the case is closed. Maybe he's stalking the Parrot Woman."

"Oh, don't mention her." I groaned. "Has Stanwyck said anything?" I asked tentatively.

"Haven't seen our ace detective. We were at the loft this morning, but she didn't make an appearance."

"Probably busy sharpening her steak knives," I told him. I didn't know what I'd do if she was still imagining herself a bird in that grisly aviary.

My mother insisted on accompanying me to the press conference. "I've known Mel Baum for years. It would be rude of me to stay away. I want the world to see that I support him fully."

"Now that he's been cleared," I murmured.

When we got out of the elevator on the seventeenth floor, I saw Lou and Mr. Sheldon going over their notes together. They looked very official, carrying black attaché cases and talking seriously. I waved to them and introduced Mother.

"You all must be very proud. Clearing poor Mel in less than a week. Of course, it must be easier to clear a client of false charges than of true ones." Mom pulled off her gloves and unbuttoned her coat.

"Much easier." Mr. Sheldon laughed loudly, thinking she'd made a joke.

"Couldn't have done it without your daughter," Lou told her.

"Whatever do you mean?" asked Mother, peering at me. "You and Stanwyck weren't getting underfoot? You promised me, Justine— "

"Lou was being polite, Mom. I had nothing to do with the case." I signaled Lou with my fiercest warning look.

"Everyone worried together," Lou said mildly.

Then Stanwyck turned up. "Hi, Jess. Ray Brown said he'd called you. Morning, Mrs. Graham. Nice of you to come."

Stanwyck sounded like her normal self, but her eyes were dark and smudged. There were webby lines on her face, as if she hadn't slept in a few nights. I squeezed her hand and said, "Maybe we can have lunch, just the two of us, after this thing is over. I know! We can go to that place in the East Village and see if their sweater sale is still on. As if we'd stopped the clock for a week."

"Another time," Stanwyck said. "The Beak is bringing over some books." She avoided my gaze.

"I'm going downstairs to the newsstand to get some hard candies," announced my mother. We walked over to the elevator to wait with her.

"Don't be too long, Mrs. G. I suspect this whole thing will be a flash in the pan. About three sentences' worth," advised Stanwyck, suddenly bossy and in control again.

The elevator opened, and out stumbled the Beak. "Isn't it great news, Jess? Stan's dad and I are regaining our freedom at the same time." He shrugged good-naturedly. "Worth a celebration, I figure."

"Beak's been calling me whenever his mother quits the surveillance for a few necessary errands. He's been reading to me all about bird history." Stan flushed. "It's like lullabyes."

"I was afraid to call you about today, Simon," I said, trying to break the aura of romantic birdiness that was hovering around us.

"Join the club, Jess. Everyone's afraid of Mama Vulture. Isn't Noah here yet? He told me they'd be starting this thing on time and that I'd better not cause a scene by coming in late." His neck thrust out. I imagined him as a tame Road Runner cartoon bird and groaned aloud.

"What's the matter?" The Beak cocked his head to one side and blinked.

"I need a few days' vacation. Everyone looks like birds to me."

"Excellent!" The Beak seemed gratified. "It's contagious, isn't it?"

"No more bird talk," said Stanwyck in her most ominous tone. She walked a few steps from us, her head dropped to her chest, and her shoulders rolled forward. I shivered. She was imitating Felicity Licht. Just as quickly, she straightened up and came back to us, her face one eager smile.

"I wish you'd been with me when she took me into the aviary, Beak."

"No bird prisons for me," he declared.

"It wasn't like that. The birds fly around quite freely. Standing amid them you feel as if you could hop onto one of those perches and crack seeds yourself."

The Beak took a deep breath. "You're learning about air. Humans left the water to the fishes aeons ago; we live in the air, yet no one is conscious of it." He leaned toward Stanwyck and began speaking rapidly, as if he were afraid someone would cut off his speech. "There are more than a hundred billion birds—fifty for each person alive—and yet nobody notices birds, except for the pretty ones."

I looked around nervously. The Beak was moving his arms up and down like wings. "Where are your parents, Stan?" I asked, gently placing my hand on the Beak's arm to quiet him. "We should join them."

"They're in the prosecutor's office," she said shortly, her eyes not leaving the Beak's face. "Would you come with me someday to the aviary, if Dr. Flyte can arrange it? The air is pure there."

"Let's find your parents." My voice had a desperate edge. This bird talk was unnerving.

Stanwyck turned to me impatiently. "They'll come out with the prosecutor and the lawyers. They're rehearsing graciousness now. It's not quite as impromptu as the news reports will make it appear."

Down the hall, TV crews were setting up their equipment. Fewer than half the people who had been jockeying for position on the street outside the loft to cover the arrest were there today. Apologies aren't news.

The elevator doors opened, and Thomas got out, followed by a gray-haired man in jeans and a cowboy hat. "He looks familiar, Stan."

She squinted at the man and grabbed my hand. "It's the creep who dumped the feathers. Mr. Ecology." She tugged at the Beak's sleeve. "Go lay some parrot talk on him, Beak. See if you can find out where he's coming from."

I had an uneasy feeling. "Stan, it's all over. We're here for the apology that will put a lid on this business."

"I don't like loose ends." She gave the Beak a light shove

in the direction of the man, who seemed to be checking out the crowd. I wondered if he was as disappointed at the turnout as I was.

The Beak went over to the man; his face was flushed and eager. "Didn't I see you on TV? You're from—I forget the name—" He held his head to one side.

"I don't give interviews," the guy said rudely, and pushed past the Beak.

Pausing a moment to regain his equilibrium, the Beak followed him a few steps down the hall. "I'm a member of Downwind."

"I don't follow rock groups," the guy sneered.

"Downwind isn't a rock group!" cried the Beak. "It's the most successful bird-activist group worldwide."

Thomas hurried over. "What's all this commotion?" He put a restraining hand on the Beak's chest. "You kids aren't supposed to be here. If you don't want the marshals to put you out, you'd better stop hassling members of the press."

Stanwyck went over and eyed him coolly. "You're off the case, so to speak. Neither the press nor you are running this show. So back off."

While we were arguing, the ecology creep left through the door to the fire stairs. Ray Brown strode toward us, his arms filled with a stack of papers. "Copies of the press release. They'll read the apology from this sheet, and then your father will make some bland statement assuring them that he's glad to live in a country where the cops own up to their mistakes. Slam, dunk, and everyone goes home happy."

Thomas's anger seemed to burn out as quickly as it had started. "Sorry for reading you kids the riot act, Stanwyck," he said, all smoothness and charm. "I guess I need about four days of R&R to become normal again."

She turned to me as if he hadn't spoken. "Let's go into the room so we can hear Daddy."

About ten reporters were standing around the room. There was a bowl of white flowers on the desk next to a small American flag. A picture of the President hung on the wall behind the desk.

We sat in the last row of chairs, piling our coats onto a chair to reserve it for Mom. In a few minutes the cameras were in position. Mr. and Mrs. Baum walked into the room and sat at the desk, and David Sheldon stood behind them. He had the stiff, solemn expression of a headwaiter at a very expensive restaurant.

As soon as the room was quiet, a tall man with very curly black hair entered the room. He looked at no one. "Last Friday morning at eleven o'clock, agents of this office arrested Mr. Mel Baum of 59 Spring Street, accusing him of operating a bird-smuggling operation with nationals of Brazil and Venezuela. We have determined that this arrest was premature, and we sincerely regret any inconvenience or embarrassment that this procedure may have caused Mr. Baum or his family."

Mrs. Baum had a plastic smile on her face. Her fingers played with her pearl necklace. She seemed half-asleep.

I was disappointed. I had expected the apology to come from the smug federal agent who'd accused Mr. Baum last week. You'd think he'd have to appear on camera. It seemed as if Mr. Baum had a right to watch him squirm.

As Mel Baum stood up to speak, there was a commotion in

the back of the room. The ecology guy had returned, carrying a large lavender-blue bird in a cage. "A cheap publicity stunt," muttered Ray Brown. "Some guys will seize any opportunity to taunt the press."

"Can't you get him out of here?" I asked. "It's not fair to Mr. Baum."

"Since last Friday morning, when federal agents burst into my apartment and I was accused of operating a bird-smuggling ring, my family has lived through a nightmare. I'd like to set the record straight. I am a New York businessman. I take very few vacations. I've never even dreamed of going to Brazil."

The guy carried the birdcage to the front of the room and sat down in a chair directly in front of Mr. Baum.

"What's wrong with Daddy?" Stanwyck jumped to her feet.

Mr. Baum had stopped speaking, as if his mind had suddenly gone blank. He blinked, rubbed his eyes, and stared off into space.

"I am a New York businessman. I'd like to set the record straight."

The bird cawed and screamed from its cage, causing a stir among the reporters. The cameramen moved in closer on the bird hopping around in its cage. Mr. Baum stared at the bird, fascinated. His wife tapped his arm. He looked at her and glanced around the room, as if trying to remember something.

"I was approached in my office late one evening almost two years ago by a Brazilian national. In exchange for receiving the crates of live birds in my warehouse until they could be shipped discreetly to points throughout the country, I was paid twenty percent of the gross in American dollars."

The room exploded. Stanwyck ran up to her father, but he seemed unaware of what a startling statement he'd made. The reporters came alive, and the crew members pointed their cameras like swollen spaceguns at Mr. Baum.

"Who was the Brazilian?"

"How many birds were shipped a month?"

"Where did you meet this Brazilian?"

"Can you identify other dealers?"

David Sheldon put his hand over the microphone. "We will have no further statements at this time!" he shouted over the reporters' questions. "I must caution you about using this statement. Mr. Baum has been under a great deal of strain. There is no indication that this confession is accurate."

The bird squawked and beat his wings against the metal wires of his cage.

Stanwyck and her mother were in tears, hugging each other. I looked around for my own mother, but she was standing in the doorway on the other side of the room. There was such pandemonium, I couldn't even signal to her. The rude ecologist brushed past her with his bulky birdcage. Two reporters followed close behind him, and when I looked around again, Mother was nowhere to be seen.

Mr. Baum still had that glazed look on his face, staring off into space. One of the reporters finally got his attention. "Where is your Brazilian contact now? Will you be turning state's evidence?"

"What Brazilian national?" he seemed to be tuning in for the first time.

104

"The one you cut the deal with. The one who arranged to use your warehouse." Questions flew from the reporters to Mr. Baum.

"Is this some kind of joke?" he asked angrily.

"You'd know that better than anyone," one of the reporters remarked.

"Stan, let's get your dad out of here." I was close to tears myself.

Chapter Eight

Strange as it seems, it was easier to get Mr. Baum released on bail now that he had confessed than it had been when the agents had first arrested him. We hadn't been back at the loft more than an hour before he and Mr. Sheldon arrived, followed by Ray Brown and Lou.

"Daddy, how could you lie to us?" cried Stanwyck. "How could you help those men steal beautiful birds from the jungle?"

"I didn't, Stanwyck. I don't know what made me invent all that business in the prosecutor's office. I've given them full permission to go over every inch of our factory without waiting for a search warrant. Mel Baum has nothing to hide. You have my word, sweetheart. No birds have ever been hidden there."

"Who's going to believe you now?" Mrs. Baum twisted her hands in front of her. "What are we going to do?" She looked at the lawyer and said in a very quiet tone, "Will they send him to jail? I don't think I can survive Mel going to jail."

"If the confession holds up—" Mr. Sheldon sighed.

"I don't remember any of the details of that confession." Mel threw his hands into the air. "If they hadn't asked me to sign that transcript later, I still wouldn't know what I said. It's like a dream. A Brazilian forcing me into smuggling birds? Get serious, I make mattresses. Maybe I don't use the best quality feathers and down, but I'm no criminal."

"Why didn't you say that to the cameras?" wailed his wife.

"Loretta, believe me, there's never been a bird, much less hundreds of them, in the factory *ever*. I can't explain it."

I walked to the end of the room and looked out at the street. A moment later, Ray Brown joined me. "I've seen guilt do strange things to people," he said in a tone barely above a whisper. His hair fell forward onto his forehead, making him look much younger and less like a lawyer. "Guilt about one thing can make you confess to another. After a major crime, police precincts are flooded with confessions. People who don't know one single detail about the actual crime will go to jail insisting they committed the crime."

"I've known Mr. Baum since I was a little girl. He's not confessing to some other secret crime. I'd have suspected if he was involved in a crooked business. Stanwyck would have known. She used to go over to the factory in Queens with him practically every weekend. She'd have noticed if there were parrots hidden under cloths. They're not exactly the quietest creatures."

"These men weren't amateurs, Watson," he said gently. "It looks like Mel Baum's been deceiving those closest to him for years."

My stomach twisted into knots at his words. "It's impossible," I insisted. "He's Stanwyck's father, not some sleazy gangster."

"It's odd that he won't tell us how the group operated. We are his attorneys. If he won't be straight with us, we're never going to be able to cut a deal with the prosecutors. He claims he can't remember the details. Probably repressed it all in an effort to convince himself he's not guilty." Ray Brown raked his hands through his hair. "It was the wildest performance I've ever seen."

Noah came to the door of the living area and motioned to me to follow him into Stanwyck's room. He smiled hesitantly. His pale face was tight with fear. "Mr. Sheldon let me in. I hope it's okay. Will you tell me what's going on? Has some disaster happened?" He bit his lip. "Is Stanwyck okay?"

"Mr. Baum confessed to smuggling the parrots in front of all those TV cameras." I looked at him resentfully. "If you'd been there on time, you'd have witnessed the whole horrible scene. Where have you been all day?"

"I was hung up on the trains. We stalled between stations for hours this morning. When I finally got to the address Stanwyck gave me, I saw that red-haired lawyer getting into a car with some loony guy in a cowboy hat carrying a birdcage. It seemed like the whole show was over, so I took the next train back up here to the loft, figuring I'd catch up with you all here. Well, I waited almost an hour before any of you showed up. And then Stanwyck got out of the cab crying, and her mother was weeping, covering her face with her hands. Nobody noticed me standing next to the door, so

I walked around the block a few times. I didn't know what else to do."

It was the longest speech Noah had ever made. He wiped the perspiration from his forehead. "Is he going to jail?"

"I guess so. It was awful, Noah. He confessed to working with a guy from Brazil. He admitted they kept the birds in his factory."

"What made him confess all of a sudden? I mean, why there, in front of the cameras? He could have confessed here, privately. That's what I would have done. No way would I have spilled the story in front of the whole world like that. Now he doesn't even have a chance to change his story. His lawyers might as well pack it in. They've got him on tape."

Stanwyck strode into the room and threw herself down onto the bed. "What are you two doing in here? Whispering about my father, trying to figure out how many years he'll get?"

"Of course not. Noah pointed out something very interesting. Your father confessed in front of zillions of witnesses instead of privately. Why?"

"Why confess at all?" she asked. "If he really did smuggle those birds, why did he wait till he'd been cleared to incriminate himself?"

"Guilty conscience?" suggested Noah.

"You believe he smuggled parrots? My *father*?" shouted Stanwyck.

"Your father believes it," I said quietly.

"We've got to clear him," she said, a determined set to her chin.

It seemed the wrong moment to remind her that he'd confessed without any prodding from the prosecutor. Even if Mr. Baum couldn't provide the details of the smuggling operation, the confession would be enough to convict him. As Ray Brown had said, people actually go to jail because of crimes they've only confessed to. The evidence is secondary to a detailed confession, no matter how false it may be.

"Where's the Beak? Did he make it to the office?" asked Noah.

"He went with my mother to the market to pick up some company food. Unfortunately, some friends of the Baums' were planning to drop by this afternoon to celebrate the prosecutor's public apology."

Stanwyck moaned and buried her face in the pillow. "I am never going outside this house again."

There was a knock on the door. "Stanwyck!" called Lou. "There's someone here to see you. She won't come inside; she's waiting by the elevator."

"I don't want to see anyone."

"You go tell her to fly away." Lou's wry amusement was clear even through the closed door. "She's got a sharp face, sort of like a crow. Wouldn't even look at me directly. She's brought this gigantic birdcage—"

Stanwyck was out the bedroom door and running through the loft. I followed, knowing as she did who was waiting on the other side of the door.

Stanwyck and Felicity stood in the hall not speaking. The cage was almost four feet high. I wondered how Felicity had managed to carry it down those narrow flights of stairs from the third-floor aviary and across Terrapin Circle.

"Sorry for your trouble," she said without expression. "I thought the macaw might comfort you."

I was astonished by the bird. He almost filled the cage; his body seemed very long. The narrow glossy tail feathers must have been two feet in length. The bird was a deep, rich hyacinth blue, a color that glowed even in the poor light of the hallway. Around his eyes and underneath his beak, the skin was bright yellow. He had a massive and powerful black beak and black feet. He sat on his perch, silent and surprisingly placid for a bird of such enormous size. I had never seen such a magnificent bird. Even if I never saw him again, I'd never forget the deep velvety violet blue of his body and the splendor of his pointed, glistening tail feathers.

Stanwyck continued to stare at the macaw, as if she were drawing strength from its hyacinth glow.

"In the sunlight I think they are the most magnificent of birds. They seem to be lit from within," Felicity said as the tips of her fingers stroked the macaw's beak through the bars of the cage. Her fingers had a tapering sweep similar to the bird's graceful tail feathers.

I had to lean forward to catch Felicity's words. She was speaking directly to Stanwyck, who was only a few inches away from her. Wrapped in her black lusterless raincoat, she was a stark contrast to the electric macaw. Her lips barely moved; she seemed almost afraid of being heard. When she had to communicate in words to humans, I noticed, her voice was lighter, airier than the strong, confident sounds that burst from her in the aviary. The splendid macaw seemed to have more strength than the woman, light as a stick, standing next to its cage.

"I couldn't. He's too exquisite. He belongs with you," stammered Stanwyck, who never took her eyes from the macaw.

Felicity did not respond to Stanwyck's confusion. She simply thrust her hand into her raincoat pocket and pulled out a plastic bag filled with seeds. "It's a good mix. Make sure he has plenty of clean water. He will bathe in the mornings in a shallow pan. Put a few fronds of fern in the pan with his bath water. He likes leaves."

"I'd be too frightened to keep him. He must be very valuable."

Felicity frowned for a moment. Then she shook her head and smiled gently. "He's priceless. He's a Hyacinth Macaw."

"I couldn't," Stanwyck stammered.

"It's all right." She touched Stanwyck's hand and spoke to her as if she were a bird. "He won't go light, and neither will you."

"What does that mean?" I asked sharply.

Surprised by my presence, Stanwyck turned around.

Felicity was startled. Her eyes grew wide, and she spun around, looking for a place to hide. "Please wait!" I cried.

Felicity tucked her head into her chest, as if she were searching for something inside her raincoat. She got into the open elevator and turned the key to descend, leaving us alone in the hallway with the Hyacinth Macaw.

"We'll have to take it back to her." I approached the cage.

Stanwyck nodded. "Let's wait till the morning. I'd love to spend a few hours with him. What an extraordinary way to get a sense of bird!" She sighed. "Like the fulfillment of a dream I didn't know I had."

112

"Will you quit this bird business? You're beginning to give me the creeps." I turned and held the door while Stanwyck cautiously lifted the cage and brought it inside the loft.

"Where do you think I should put him? My room is too small."

"Near the window at the other end of the living room, overlooking the street, where he'll get the sun in the morning," I suggested.

"There might be a draft from that huge window. The east wind is fierce this time of year. Maybe near the radiator. Oh dear, I don't know how warm he's supposed to be. He needs to live in Felicity's aviary, where it's safe." Stanwyck set the cage on the floor and sat next to it on the couch. I handed her the plastic bag of seeds. She sprinkled a few into the palm of her hand but did not thrust her hand into the cage.

"Be careful, Stan. That beak looks like it could mince rock. Happily."

She closed her fingers over the seeds. "You're right. That woman is insane. I don't know anything about birds!"

"Stop being so tragic. Sprinkle the seeds on the floor of the cage. She wouldn't have given you such a precious bird if it would do him harm," I began in my reasonable, logical tone. "Those birds are her life." Stanwyck's eyes met mine. We were both thinking of the little brown bags on the sidewalk beside the idling car. We looked away, and neither of us said a word.

Ray Brown joined us on the couch to admire the macaw. "What a creature!" The macaw seemed to sense we were gazing at him. He threw back his head, exposing the vivid

113

yellow of his throat. Slowly he rotated his neck and preened, puffing up his body feathers.

Ray looked at me with undisguised curiosity. "A gift from the Parrot Woman?"

"You got it. Delivered in person."

"You must have made quite an impression," Ray Brown said to Stanwyck. "You'll have to train me in your technique of interrogating witnesses."

"She had watched the news conference on TV," I said, putting my hand on his arm to restrain his teasing manner.

"I'm never going to school again," said Stanwyck quietly.

Ray Brown leaned across the macaw's cage and spoke to Stanwyck. His tone was serious. "Listen to me. Your father is in his study going over every minute of the press conference with Lou. They taped the TV coverage on the VCR. He still insists he's innocent and that he doesn't know what made him say he had a Brazilian black-market contact." He shrugged and tapped lightly on the cage bar with his fingernail. "Personally, against all my lawyerly training, I'm inclined to believe him. I don't know what made him confess. Maybe we'll never know. A momentary aberration. But there's a strong possibility that we can get him cleared of all charges. There's no tangible evidence of any actual connection, since those phone numbers in Bahia and Caracas are dead ends. Y'all did a very creditable job, illuminating that 800-phone crack. Actually, I think the feds are set to go galloping off after the phreakers. If Mr. Baum retracts the confession—"

"You see, Stanwyck? It's going to be all right!" In my excitement, I kicked the cage. The macaw squawked and flapped his wings. His lidless round black eye glared at me

114

balefully. He flapped and struck at the cage bars with his beak. "Quick, Stan, some seeds! Before he crushes me into penny candy."

Stanwyck threw a handful of mixed seeds onto the floor of the macaw's cage. The macaw hopped down and sorted through the seeds until he found a black-skinned one. He cracked it in his beak and dropped the hard shell to the ground. Then he picked up a seed that looked flat, like granola, and an instant later spat out its tan shell. It was thrilling to watch how he could separate the seed shell from its fruit with only his beak—no hands, no fingers.

Losing interest in the pile of seeds, he sprang up, with a slight flick of his wings, onto his perch and eyed us; first with his left eye, then with his right. Under that softness of hyacinth feathers was a powerful body. He moved with the sureness of an athlete.

"Your father has been over every inch of that tape. What did we all do before freeze frame?" said Lou. He sat on the couch and handed a legal pad full of notes to Ray Brown without noticing the macaw. As if resenting the shift of attention away from himself, the macaw, sitting on his perch, squawked and ruffled his feathers. "Where did that come from?" asked Lou, leaning forward to examine the macaw more closely.

"The Parrot Woman, the one with the aviary across the street. The girls went to see her about possible connections to the genuine bird smugglers. Well, she heard the conference on TV and brought the bird over to cheer us up." Ray Brown leaned over, resting his elbows on his knees. "A dynamite bird."

"Funny thing, he looks a bit like the one at the press conference."

"Nonsense," said Stanwyck. "The cages make them seem alike."

"No," I said slowly, "that bird was blue, too."

"There is no connection," said Stanwyck firmly. She picked up the cage. "I've decided to keep him in my room tonight. It'll be a bit snug, but I'll feel better with him next to the bed."

"Where did that cage come from?" Mr. Baum called from the doorway at the other end of the loft. "That's some big bird."

"Come look, Daddy. It's a Hyacinth Macaw. Felicity brought him to me."

"Who's Felicity?"

"I'll tell you all about her later. He cracks seeds in his beak." Stanwyck put the cage on the floor and danced over to her father. She put her arms around his neck. "I'm sorry I was such a prune. Of course you didn't steal birds and hide them at the factory. I never truly doubted you." Her voice was high-pitched. She was talking in a singsong voice like a little girl.

The macaw squawked and beat his wings against the cage bars. Mr. Baum's attention was caught by the bird. He moved closer, stared at the deep violet-blue wings, and rubbed his eyes. A moment later he sighed deeply.

"I was approached in my office late one evening almost two years ago by a Brazilian national. In exchange for receiving the crates of live birds in my warehouse until they could

116

be shipped discreetly to points throughout the country, I was paid twenty percent of the gross in American dollars."

Stanwyck's scream filled the loft—an unholy sound. It sent shivers up my spine. It set off the macaw, who squawked repeatedly and beat his wings against the bars of his cage. The bird's wings were so strong that Ray Brown had to steady the iron cage with both arms. Lou attempted to calm the bird, while I tried to comfort Stanwyck. Oddly, Mr. Baum seemed unaware that he'd been the cause of his daughter's hysteria. After he finished delivering his confession for the second time that day, he continued to look up at the ceiling as if he had been reading from a script printed there.

Stanwyck threw herself facedown onto the couch, weeping. The sound of her sobs triggered the macaw. Nearly human crying noises erupted from the cage. The bird's sounds were higher and had a tighter, almost choking sound to them. His cries grew more desperate; I wondered if he'd learned to imitate such cries from listening to TV soap operas. All the commotion brought Mrs. Baum into the living room. Seeing Stanwyck in tears, she ran to her husband, sat on the arm of his chair, and leaning against his chest, began to sob.

Suddenly, the loft was filled with shrieks of despair. I sat on the couch next to Stanwyck's quivering body and covered my ears with my hands. Shaking his head in amazement, Ray Brown took the birdcage into Stanwyck's room to get the macaw away from the stimulus of her sobs and closed the door.

Unable to cope with Stanwyck, I hurried after Ray. "What do you think made Mr. Baum repeat his confession?" I asked. "After insisting he was innocent, he did another about-face. I don't understand any of this."

The macaw stood on the floor of the cage spitting out seeds. Noah, lying on his stomach, was almost at eye level with the bird. "It's uncanny. He could be the same bird as the one I saw being put into that cab outside the court house this morning." He looked up at me impishly. "Maybe they're twins."

"You say you've seen this bird before?" Ray Brown sat on Stanwyck's rumpled bed. "That's interesting. I wonder if the bird is somehow connected to the confession."

"You mean he's one of the smuggled birds? When Mr. Baum sees him, his guilt is triggered?" I asked, feeling utterly brilliant. "The bird will lead us to the real smugglers."

"We should get a psychologist in here. I know just the one." Ray left the room without acknowledging my having given him the key.

Stanwyck came into her room, supported by Noah. She looked as frail as a rag doll. With his arm around her shoulders, Noah seemed older. "Beak's here. Stanwyck couldn't listen to him rave about the Hyacinth Macaw."

"Let him see the bird, Stan. Without him we'd never have known about Felicity, and we'd never have the macaw in the first place."

"And my father might not have confessed. Isn't that what you're thinking?" Stanwyck turned on me angrily.

"Of course not." I hurried out of the room to get the Beak. If nothing else, he'd serve as a buffer to the frantic Stanwyck.

Noah was frowning at the ceiling. "Hey, Beak. How many of these macaws could there be in the city, anyway?"

"Yeah, Beak. Isn't there some way to find out—"

"I'm way ahead of you. We'll call Dr. Flyte. He must have some sort of listing. Thanks to the presence of the macaw, doors will be opened to us that wouldn't otherwise be. We can use the Parrot Woman to our advantage."

"Nobody is going to bother Felicity." Stanwyck roused herself and glared fiercely at each of us in turn.

"Of course not," said the Beak in a soothing, birdy tone. "But when Dr. Flyte hears that the Parrot Woman has given you a rare Hyacinth Macaw, he'll help us in any way he can. Depend on it."

Stan looked like a candidate for one of the Parrot Woman's little brown bags. She curled up on her bed and stared at the macaw. Curiously, the bird had picked up on her mood and sat hunched, his head under his wing. The Beak sat on the edge of Stanwyck's bed trying to comfort her. From time to time his attention was absorbed by the bird. Since he felt himself to be more bird than human, being so close to a rare bird almost engulfed him.

Finally, I tapped the Beak on his shoulder. "Dr. Flyte?" I reminded him gently.

"The Parrot Woman's name is surely magic." The Beak had a glazed look on his face. We were in a taxi going to 6½ Montague Street because Monty Flyte, a rare bird himself, had agreed to meet us and his brother at his house at the tip end of Manthattan. "I should have figured there would be

119

some sort of centralized databank." The Beak chewed his thumbnail.

"Do all birdy people live in town houses?" I asked as the cab pulled up at the address we'd given him.

"Only the rich ones," the Beak remarked.

Like Felicity, Monty Flyte opened the door a sliver and inspected us bird-style, first with his left eye, then with his right.

"Come in, please, come in." He hung up our coats in an almost-empty closet. Its doorknob was a painted robin red-breast on a budding branch. "It's been a while since I've seen Felicity, but of course, one keeps up. There isn't an avicul-turist anywhere in the world who could not describe her collection. And yet who has actually seen it?"

"I have," I said quickly. "She has beautiful parrots."

Mr. Flyte peered at me. "You are the one with Felicity's Hyacinth Macaw."

"No, sir, that's my friend Stanwyck. Felicity Licht gave the bird to her." I tried to keep the impatience out of my voice. My intuition informed me that Mr. Flyte was a talker who welcomed the opportunity. We weren't going to get any information until he was good and ready to provide it.

"My brother Winnie has been delayed, but he assures me you young people are most capable. He doesn't use that word lightly. My brother is a serious fellow—always was. When we were at school he'd read dark poetry about death. He was bad at school, you know. Stumped by history and literature. Just a steady diet of poems about starvation and death. Of course, his devotion to taxidermy is a way of fooling death. So lifelike when he's finished." I cast a wor-

120

ried glance at the Beak. Monty Flyte's singsong voice filled the room. He had no sense of the urgency of our mission.

The room we stood in was dark, with heavy wood furniture. The couch and window drapes were covered with a gray and brown pattern of long-tailed pheasants. On the walls hung framed portraits of birds. A couple of deep leather chairs were drawn close to the fireplace. Bird-shaped andirons held neatly piled logs. In one corner of the room, a huge desk with legs carved like flying eagles was piled with computer print-outs.

"I have so much desk work." The old man caught me glancing at his piles of papers. "Paper work all morning—that's a man's lot in life, my father used to tell us. What a man he was. He had a natural understanding of other people's situations. Others, including dear Mother, were horrified by Winnie's fascination with dead animals. But Father encouraged him to learn taxidermy, the simplest entry into his craft. Well, it breathed life into my brother. Those vacations were his lifeline. Not just birds, but moles and voles, and a twelve-pound water muskrat one summer." He chuckled.

Remembering the museum workroom, I shivered slightly. "I prefer birds breathing," I said, hoping he'd lead us to the aviary. "We have so little time to find if there are other Hyacinth Macaws in New York."

"What Jess means is that she's not familiar with the important contribution of taxonomists and aviculturists to species survival."

"It's no black mark to prefer living species." Mr. Flyte

smiled at me. "To encounter a Rose-Winged Cockatoo is to glimpse Eden."

The Beak scanned the room. Our eyes met. "Where are the birds?" I whispered, as the old man led us through a small doorway and down a long, poorly lit hall. We reached the back of the house and followed him down a flight of uncarpeted stairs into a paneled anteroom. It had the damp chill of a cellar. The Beak pointed to a barred metal doorway straight ahead. "He probably keeps them sheltered from view. These collectors are very private," he said knowledgeably.

Mr. Flyte paused at the door and fumbled with a large, rattling key ring. "One must take precautions with confidential material," he said, and threw his weight against the door.

If the pheasants on the upholstery had suddenly sprung to life, I wouldn't have been more surprised than I was by what was behind that door. On spotless white Formica platforms stood three computer terminals. The floor was of highly polished white tile, like a medical laboratory. Along the far wall was a mainframe computer. There were no windows, no pictures, no color anywhere. There was only one chair, metallic and of modern design, with a metal seat, set in front of one of the terminals. The only sound was the low hum of an air-filtering system.

The Beak was more unglued than I was. "Where are the birds?" he whined.

"Birds?" Mr. Flyte appeared puzzled. "What would I do with birds? When would I care for them? I told you, desk work all morning, then the upkeep on the files down here. Birds would be such a distraction. Look at dear Felicity. The burden of life-and-death responsibility. Never gets away from the demands of the aviary. If I kept birds"—he chuckled—"I'd be the one in the cage."

"Mr. Flyte," I said, aware that my hands were trembling, "my friend's father has been accused of a crime he has not committed. If we do not find the identity of the other macaws in this vicinity, he will most likely go to prison. We thought you could help us."

"So I can," he said, turning on the switch at the side of the smaller of the two computers, "within minutes."

He took a white handkerchief from his pocket and dusted the immaculate chair in front of him. "If you two will wait over here, we shall have the macaw information in minutes. You see, I have all the breeding lines as well as a list of all live Hyacinth Macaws in the Western Hemisphere—which is, of course, the only place one finds the lovely creatures. And then we have a databank of scholarly articles related to each species." His voice trailed off as his fingers danced across the computer keys.

"Find A—A— Beak, would you look at this sheet and tell me what the code is for the Hyacinth Macaw?"

The Beak scanned the plastic-enclosed sheet that held computer codes for several columns of bird species. "You really cover the whole spectrum," the Beak said, his voice husky with admiration.

"No, no, my boy. These are only parrots and related birds. One must specialize these days. There's an aviculturist in Nebraska who only does lorikeets. Has to call me to download any breeding or hybridizing information on macaws, conures—all the Psittacidae. Now, look under Anodor-hynchus and Ara, the major genera classifications of macaws."

"Here it is! A/13h, the Hyacinth Macaw."

I held my breath. A/13h. Within two minutes the screen began to fill up. "Here's one in Dilthey, Vermont," Mr. Flyte told us. "And here is Felicity Licht." We hurried over to read the screen over his shoulder. "It says she has two specimens," I said.

"No, my dear, she *had* two. She reported the death of one last summer. That's the %% code after the name here."

"Are you sure that's the entire updated list?" the Beak asked half an hour later as we examined the print-out. "Chadd's Ford, Pennsylvania, and Terre Haute, Indiana?"

"Absolutely." Mr. Flyte beamed. "Knowing the where-abouts of each of these rare birds is a most satisfying feeling!"

"Not for us, I'm afraid," I said. "You see, Mr. Flyte, we hoped to find at least one other bird to clear Felicity of suspicion. Since there is no other Hyacinth Macaw registered in New York, we've found evidence that will convict Stanwyck's Parrot Woman."

Chapter Nine

The list of the eight owners of Hyacinth Macaws east of the Mississippi was folded in my pocket. My hand rested on top of it. The Beak had been quiet on the way back to the loft. As we rang the Baums' doorbell, he spoke for the first time. "If we said the computer didn't produce any evidence, we wouldn't have to implicate the Parrot Woman."

"We can't fool around. This is a federal crime." The Beak groaned; I shared his discomfort. "It's hard to imagine her a bird smuggler." But I was dreading Stanwyck's grief more than the Parrot Woman's finally being caught. "Face it, Beak. Her parrot is the only one registered in New York."

"It is incriminating," he whispered as Lou let us into the loft. Ray Brown was talking to Mr. and Mrs. Baum. Noah stood apart from the group, his arms crossed in front of him. He was paying close attention to the conversation, listening for Stanwyck.

"My cousin Holly is a clinical psychologist. Not the usual stripe, old Holly. She believes in the unproved phenomena that her colleagues scoff at. Works with all kinds of unusual phenomena. Ghosts who leave scents of raspberries in the room, people who can predict car crashes halfway across the globe—that sort of thing. I'm going to give her a call. I don't want to conclude anything until I check it out with a pro."

"You think this might clear Mr. Baum"—my heart beat faster—"without tracing the owner of the macaw?"

"Let's just say, Watson, that Mr. Baum may not be the swine he appears to be." He went to the living room to call the woman who would turn Stan's father back into a human.

She'd better be a magician as well as a psychologist, I thought as Lou locked the door behind us.

"Nothing less than a miracle will get Mr. Baum to stop these confessions," Lou whispered to me. He seemed too discouraged for me to tell him that our news wasn't radiant, either. Lou was explaining to the Beak what had transpired in our absence. "Until Sheldon's sure, he won't let loose again with one of his confessions out of the blue. He's going to keep him sealed away from the public. No contact with anyone, much less the prosecutors, who aren't exactly on his side to begin with. The biggest hope is Ray's cousin, but some judges won't admit parapsychological testimony."

I motioned to Noah and the Beak to follow me into Stanwyck's room.

Once in the room, Noah seemed possessed by the macaw. He tapped the cage bars, making low *chirrup* sounds. The macaw hopped over to him. He made little contented sounds deep in his throat. Noah placed some seeds on the tips of his fingers and reached through the cage bars toward the bird.

"Don't do that. He could snap off your fingers like candy canes," I warned.

126

"Not this beauty," said Noah. To my surprise, the bird gently nibbled at the seeds, coyly rolling his head to the side, staring at Noah almost flirtatiously through his right eye.

Noah opened the door of the cage but did not attempt to remove the macaw. I lay on the bed watching the two of them. The macaw uttered a peep and stood his ground. Gradually he hopped toward his water dish, which was near the open part of the cage. He dipped his head into the dish, drank a few drops, and then ruffled out his feathers. In a flurry of wings, he flew to his perch. While all this was going on, Noah didn't move a muscle. The macaw waited a moment, hopped back to the floor of the cage, and hopped toward the opening. He stretched out his neck and laid his head on Noah's hand.

Noah stroked the bird's beak. "I've never been so close to a bird," he whispered to me. Startled, the macaw retreated into his cage.

There was a knock on the door. I got off the bed and opened the door. "Oh my goodness! What is going on? Mel and Loretta are devastated. Totally out of control," breathed my mother. With her face reddened from the cold and her hair mussed, she didn't have the in-charge look that I connect with her. She's always combed and calm. Watching Noah and the macaw, I'd almost forgotten the disarray we'd left in the other room.

I put my arms around my mother. "Poor Mom, you got more than you bargained for. While you were shopping, Mr. Baum assured us he hadn't ever smuggled birds."

"Well, that's more like it." She sat down. "But why are they so grim?"

"A few minutes ago he repeated his confession."

"You're kidding!"

"That's what broke the bank," I said loudly.

My voice startled the macaw, who flicked his wings against the cage bars.

Mother leaned over to examine the bird. "Where did he come from? Isn't he the one that unshaven fellow was carrying at the court house?"

"That's what Noah said." I was surprised that they both remembered the bird from this morning. I had a dim recollection of a birdcage, but I hadn't noticed the bird inside the cage.

"I rode up in the elevator with him. I'm positive it was a blue bird. I thought to myself, what an exquisite color, like the sky on a July night at dusk. I used to have a dress nearly that shade when you were a little girl." Mom sighed. "That red-haired young lawyer was talking to the ecologist—"

"When? Where?" demanded Stanwyck, sitting up, suddenly alert. Her face looked creased, as if she'd just woken from a restless sleep.

"In the elevator to the press conference."

"That's very interesting," said Stanwyck, leaning over to close the cage door. "I don't want him flying around. We can't stand any extra confusion." She picked up her hairbrush. "Mr. Sheldon can't remember ever sending Thomas here. He thought the third person working on the case was a paralegal named Beth. And she was the liaison from the office."

"Then where did Thomas come from?" I asked.

"Isn't that the question?" Stanwyck rebraided her hair and smiled at me.

"He certainly sounded like a lawyer. But if he were an imposter, wouldn't Ray Brown and Lou have picked up on it? They were all working together!"

"He may well be a lawyer but not for Sheldon's firm. He was sent here to keep an eye on my father." Even as she said those words, it was clear from her sad expression that the words came more from her sense of drama than from any actual evidence.

"You mean, find the redhead and you find the real smugglers?" I asked.

"That is most unlikely," said Noah. He had squinched himself into the corner with his arms around his legs. His unhappy face made it clear that he was uncomfortable about disagreeing with Stanwyck. "Don't pin your hopes—"

Ray Brown came into the room and laughed. "Are you all trying to win the Guinness book for most people squashed into a minuscule space with a birdcage?"

"Did Mr. Sheldon find out any more information about Thomas?" Stanwyck asked, banging her shin on the birdcage.

Ray Brown laughed. "We've got someone posted at his apartment, someone else at the office. He's bound to turn up. But you're grasping at straws. He knows his case law, and he worked all night on the tax records. Partners never know the scrub teams in firms as large as ours. Don't go expecting a criminal behind every legal pad," he said in his most patronizing tone.

Stanwyck glowered at him. "Let's get out of here, Jess. I

feel as if we're in the cage; the bird's the only one who's got enough room."

"I'll stay here," said Noah as we followed Stanwyck into the living room. Another convert for birdiness, I thought to myself. The macaw was lovely to look at for a few minutes, but personally I couldn't see what all the excitement was about.

"There must be real smugglers, somebody who wants my father to appear to be a smuggler," Stanwyck announced when we were all seated. My mother was in the kitchen area fixing one tray of coffee and tea and another one of tea cakes. Mrs. Baum sat next to her husband, her hand on top of his. She hadn't said a word all afternoon.

"Daddy, I know it's that Thomas." She glared at Ray Brown. "*They* won't believe me."

"It's hard to believe, darling. After all, he took me to the dentist and waited with me. At the hourly rate, I suspect, but he was gracious and concerned about my pain. There's no denying the boy's been helpful. But if you have a hunch—" He sat up straighter. "Call your personnel people, Sheldon. We'll know in a minute if he's a member of the firm," Mr. Baum suggested.

"There are two possibilities that come immediately to mind. He's either a journalist for a scummy gossiping rag posing as an attorney—" Mr. Sheldon was already preparing a case against Thomas.

"He knew his case law and actually gave us some excellent leads." Ray Brown was not going to convict him so easily.

"He worked late several nights helping me get the tax

records in order for the prosecutor's office," Lou reminded us.

"Why would he have done that if he were working for some imagined enemy?" Mr. Baum asked. He looked utterly defeated, with great dark circles under his eyes; his face was ashen. He slouched against the pillows of the couch as if he had been anesthetized. "I'm done for. We're clutching at straws." With his stomach puffed out over his belt, he sagged as if he were a doll whose stuffing was leaking out.

"No, Daddy, don't give up. You didn't do this." Stanwyck's voice was flat. She seemed to be forcing out the words.

"Maybe somebody put a spell on him," I said, only half joking.

Stanwyck started to say something, then remained silent.

"That may not be off the mark," said Ray Brown quietly.

Stan narrowed her eyes. "I wouldn't believe you if you said birds had wings."

"Coffee and tea," said my mother with a stiff smile on her face. I went to the kitchen and carried out the second tray for her. I couldn't remember whether she had ever been at the Baums' loft. Whenever she mentions Stanwyck's parents or sees them at school functions, she seems to be making an effort to be pleasant to them.

Mrs. Baum gazed into her cup of tea as she stirred several spoonfuls of sugar into it. Watching her, Stanwyck laughed. "Mom, you take lemon in your tea."

"I thought it was coffee," she said, resting the cup on the table.

The doorbell rang. Ray Brown jumped up to answer it. Mr. Baum rubbed his eyes and said softly, "Please don't let anyone in. I can't face people." He appealed to his wife, who didn't seem to hear him.

Ray Brown returned with his arm around the shoulders of a short, bouncy woman with frizzy blond hair. Stanwyck caught my eye and raised her eyebrows. I shrugged in response. "This is my cousin Holly. She's a psychologist, Mr. Baum, who has studied all kinds of paranormal phenomena."

"You think I'm nuts," he said without rancor.

Holly laughed and sat on a corner of the marble coffee table. "No, paranormal involves hypnotism, levitation, and all phenomena that are not deemed credible by the normal clinical field. They are happenings that cannot be proved or substantiated clinically. But intuitively or experientially, it is clear that they exist."

"You think you can explain why I confessed to a crime I didn't commit."

"I can try," she said briskly. "Ray tells me that you confessed twice today but never this morning. Is that correct?"

"Yes. I didn't even remember the confession until I saw the videotape playback. I didn't remember saying those words. And then about an hour ago, I confessed all over again."

"Do you remember the words of the confession now?"

He shook his head.

"Sounds like deep hypnosis. But to put an end to the posthypnotic suggestion, we have to find the trigger." She took out a pad. "At the press conference, do you remember any sensations, any aura, any whirling lights in front of your eyes?"

"Nothing except the lights on the TV cameras. I felt fine. A little nervous. I've been as jumpy as a cat ever since this whole nightmare began."

My mother came back into the room. "What about the bird, that dreadful man with the bird in the cage who shoved past me to get into the press conference? Rude and arrogant. Then he pushed his way all the way to the front of the room. He sat right in front of you, and I don't think he was even a reporter. How could he be, carrying that bulky cage?"

"Now that you mention it, I do remember a commotion when he entered the room. I was afraid he was going to make a speech about injuring our feathered friends—the same sort of business he pulled the day they arrested me. A real airhead, as my daughter would say." Mr. Baum smiled, and some color returned to his face.

"Does that give you any clues, Holly?" Ray Brown asked.

"What were the circumstances surrounding the second confession? Did you see the same man? Did you think about him or hear those words about the birds he spoke at the press conference?"

Mr. Baum shook his head. "Nothing. I was in my room going over the tape with Lou, and then I came out here to see what Stanwyck was so excited about."

"A Hyacinth Macaw," explained Stanwyck, "given to me by a parrot expert who lives on Terrapin Circle. But she never came inside the loft. Daddy never met her."

"Is the bird here?" asked Holly.

"In my room."

"Bring him out here when I give you the signal, in about ten minutes," Holly told her. "First I want to study the videotape to see if I can discover what triggers the confessions."

After Stanwyck went inside, Mom came over and sat next to me. "This is the most bizarre happening I can imagine," she whispered. Her eyes never left Mr. Baum's face. "I hate to leave you here, dear, but I promised your father I'd meet him for dinner in midtown. It'll take me hours to get home from here."

Poor Mom, she can't cope with strangeness or surprise. Every day is the same for her. She isn't crazy even about taking an alternate bus route to a department store. "I'll be home later, or I'll call you at nine. How's that?" I asked.

"Make my excuses to everyone, dear. Not that they'll notice, in all this confusion." Only my mother could walk unconcerned out of a room where excitement was crackling all around her. Mother's never been late for dinner.

Holly returned to the room smiling. "Now, Mr. Baum, tell me the truth. Do you know the bird smugglers?"

"Absolutely not."

Holly motioned to Stanwyck, who brought the cage and set it on the coffee table in front of her father. The macaw flicked his wings and ruffled his feathers. Mr. Baum sighed. "I must admit I was approached in my office late one evening almost two years ago by a Brazilian national. In exchange for receiving the crates of live birds in my warehouse until they could be shipped discreetly to points throughout the country, I was paid twenty percent of the gross in American dollars."

"It's the bird!" we all shouted.

The macaw squawked and began to laugh like a TV soundtrack.

"Where did he come from?"

"I told you that Parrot Woman was involved. Right from the beginning I knew she was eerie!" I insisted. "You got hung up on the birds, but remember, she was gassing them the other night."

"Jess, you promised!" cried Stanwyck. "Those birds must have been sick; she was doing the kindest thing."

"What are you girls talking about?"

As Stanwyck turned to Lou, her face took on a false smile. "Jess has this thing about Felicity. Thinks she's wicked. But she's only shy. Jess sees demonic, but Felicity's just different."

"Item, she gasses birds in the middle of the night. Item, she has the bird that sets off your father's phony confessions." I paused for breath.

"I admit it looks bad, but she can explain. She brought me the bird because he's beautiful, not because she wanted to hurt Daddy."

"Maybe she's unbalanced," suggested Lou. "When she came to the door, she could barely articulate that she wanted to know if Stanwyck lived here. She clung to that cage as if she were the bird and he were the keeper."

"Okay, she's not wrapped like every other package," conceded Stanwyck. "But that doesn't mean she's a criminal."

"Well, how do you explain your father's reaction to the bird?" demanded her mother, suddenly animated. "That old witch was prepared to send Mel to prison so she could protect her supply of birds."

Holly held up her hands for silence. "You all have to give

135

Mr. Baum some peace. If we're going to unravel this mystery, his mind has to be clear, and he has to be relaxed." She put her hand on Mr. Baum's arm and spoke gently, the way Felicity spoke to her birds. "You and I are going to go into another room, away from all these people. If you are willing, I'm going to hypnotize you to see if we can go back through the few days since this whole business began." Holly held her head to one side in imitation of the bird. "Together we'll pinpoint the circumstances of the first hypnosis and how this macaw fits into the picture."

Mr. Baum stood up and followed Holly. He slid his feet across the floor as he walked; he seemed like an animal accustomed to walking on a leash. Stanwyck stretched out on the floor next to the cage and stared at the macaw. "You like your cage, don't you, Beauty? You can see the whole world, but no one can get at you. I'm going to take you back to the aviary." Stanwyck rolled over onto her back. Her fingers were curled around the bars of the cage, a dreamy expression on her face. She seemed unaware of the rest of us. "Felicity will protect us. We'll be safe in her aviary and eat good things from the palm of her hand."

I knelt next to my friend. "Stop it, Stanwyck. You're safe right here."

She looked at me, tears seeping through her eyelashes. "I want to live in the aviary. No one knows it's there. I hate this loft. It needs walls."

"Of course there are walls here. Let's go into your room. It's small as a cage."

Stanwyck curled up next to the cage on the floor. I sat on the bed. Noah was sitting at the computer, but he stared at the blank screen, making birdy noises with his tongue. Even Noah seemed under the spell of the macaw. "I'm going to take the bird back in the morning, no matter what happens here. I know Felicity had nothing to do with it."

"The police may impound the macaw. As evidence."

Stanwyck sprang to her feet, kicking the cage. The macaw squawked. "No one is going to harm you, Beauty. I will get you back to Felicity."

"Face it, Stanwyck, she may be the one to flee. All the fingers point directly at her. I didn't want to tell you, but according to Monty Flyte's databank, she's the only one with Hyacinth Macaws in New York."

We heard a commotion in the living room and went out there. Two police investigators were standing with Thomas between them. He did not respond when Ray Brown and Mr. Sheldon asked him questions about his connection to the firm. "Call the personnel department," he said smoothly.

"We have a call into them," Mr. Sheldon warned him.

"They'll confirm my hiring date was July 12. I am a graduate of Harvard Law." He spoke patiently. "I understand the temptation to fob off the guilt, especially when the client is as personable as Mr. Baum." He smiled. "But I'm afraid I'm not your crook."

"Mom, there are two lawyers from the DA's office's here. They want us all in the living room." Stan and I helped Mrs. Baum find her sweater and her shoes. She made an attempt to tidy her hair. Could it be only three in the afternoon? I felt as if we'd been listening to possible explanations for days—explanations that fizzled just in time for the next candiate to become our favorite prime suspect.

"The DA contingent looks serious, as if they've got something tough to tell us." Stan looked more excited than frightened. "The older one was at the news conference. I remember because he has silver hair like Phil Donahue, and he wears a tight gray suit, which is more a uniform for these fellows than a regulation cop uniform."

"Don't say *cop*, dear. It's crude."

"Mom!" Stan trailed her mother out of the bedroom. "Dad is about to be hauled off to the Big House, and you're worried that I'm being crude!"

Mrs. Baum swept rather grandly into the living room. "Manners are forever. Stanwyck, Jess, get the gentlemen something cool to drink."

Stan clutched my arm. "She's playing Good Queen Bess. Ignore it. 'Get them something to drink'—after all they've put Daddy through!"

"Young man, we'd like to hear how you became involved with Mr. Baum," one of the DA lawyers took a step toward Thomas.

"This doesn't seem to be my lucky day," Thomas answered smoothly. He repeated the story he'd told us earlier, including the suggestion that they verify his story with the personnel department of Mr. Sheldon's law firm.

"Do you know Georgios Castell or Lee Telegros?"

"The names are not familiar."

"Think carefully." The silver-haired lawyer spoke severely. "Do you remember a session in the district attorney's office

138

about three months ago to discuss some importing irregularities?"

Thomas's face turned pale. He put his hands in his pockets and walked around in a small circle. "There are so many cases." He shrugged. "Perhaps."

"Perhaps reading the transcript of the meeting will help you remember this one, Mr. Lawrence Hoffmann." He put a bound pile of papers about two inches thick on the table in front of Thomas. "We have checked with the personnel department. And a Thomas Ryan, with age and background to fit all the stories you've been telling, was hired to work for Danser Whippany about eight months ago.

"But he's at least three inches shorter than you, with jet black hair. You might have gotten away with using his name if he hadn't joined the firm's jogging club. He placed among the top ten runners in the Christmas marathon. They have a picture of him crossing the finish line in his file."

Thomas sat down heavily on the couch and covered his face with his hands. My heart beat faster. Clearly we were about to hear an on-the-spot confession. Live and unrehearsed.

"I'm Larry Hoffman, and the man I was representing in your office was my uncle, Lee Telegros. He heads a worldwide importing business. When we saw the news conference about this mattress-maker caught for smuggling, we figured we had a way to drop all the suspicion from Lee. Get the feds off his back. Easier than producing a lot of phony documentation."

"How did you insinuate yourself into our law firm?" Lou asked.

Thomas ran his fingers through his hair. "The news ac-

139

counts mentioned the lawyer's name, even ran his picture alongside his client's. It was no big deal to go to the firm, ostensibly to leave off my résumé. I asked to talk to a personnel interviewer, the one who sees the prospective lawyers. The interviewer brought an empty file, and I swapped it for the Thomas Ryan file that was sitting on her desk. A little juggling—no big deal."

Stanwyck rushed forward and put her hands on Thomas's shoulders. "Was Felicity in it? Did she supply the bird?"

"That dried-up stick figure in the black raincoat? Not quite my type. Once we decided to hypnotize Mr. Baum, we needed a trigger. Someone suggested a bird, in keeping with the bird connection to the case. My next move was to convince that lunatic ecology guy that I was so bird-minded, I wouldn't eat a scrambled egg. Plus, I offered to do some free legal work for our friends the birds."

"Felicity didn't hurt us." Stanwyck ran to the window and pressed her cheek against the glass.

"I knew that ecology guy wasn't our sort of ornitho-activist." The Beak grinned. "He was too surly, too animal—you know what I mean?"

"Where did the bird come from?" Lou asked. He never lost the thread of a story once he had hold of it.

"I got the macaw from my college roommate. He lives in Pennsylvania."

I pulled out Monty Flyte's computer print-out. "Chadd's Ford?"

"How did you know?"

"You're not the only clever one," I snapped.

"Good going, Watson." Ray Brown jumped up and in his

excitement hugged me. Making the whole trip to Monty Flyte's secret computer worthwhile.

Stanwyck rejoined us. I felt as if I owed her something. "If the Parrot Woman hadn't brought the identical bird here, we would never have unraveled this case." The words didn't come easily. I was unwilling to turn that dark creature into the miracle worker of the day.

Stanwyck burst into joyous tears. "Felicity saved Dad! She didn't harm anyone."

Ray Brown frowned and put his arm around Stanwyck. He was certainly free with his hugs all of a sudden. "Let's not get too carried away. Maybe Thomas, a/k/a Lawrence, is protecting the Parrot Woman. She certainly had a motive—to get rare birds for her aviary. And she was in a perfect position to supply birds to all the other eager aviculturists in the country." Ray Brown put his fingertips together as if in prayer.

Stanwyck turned on him angrily. "That's about as reasonable as what the police are saying about my father. You can't prove they're guilty, and neither of them can prove they're innocent."

I thought of the carefully hidden computer network at Monty Flyte's house. It could certainly have served as a clearinghouse for fulfilling birdlovers' fantasies.

"I think I may be able to clear your father," Holly exclaimed, and hurried across the loft, waving her arms. "There has definitely been hypnotic suggestion. We can pinpoint it to the time of the dental appointment."

One of the policemen stepped forward. "We've heard that, miss, but what proof have you?"

"This!" Holly held up a plate of caramel candies. "When Mr. Baum bit into one, his tooth began to ache—the same tooth the dentist was supposed to have sealed. During the hypnosis, the fraudulent doctor planted the suggestion that his toothache was cured, but caramel sugar is stronger than hypnotic suggestion."

"We'll have to get a dentist to attest that the tooth is the same one Mr. Baum had thought was fixed last week and that it indeed has not been fixed." The police sergeant nodded to Mr. Sheldon. "Let's get together tomorrow morning to decide how to deal with the press on this."

"No more publicity. I want to go back to making mattresses," sighed Mr. Baum.

The macaw stared at the floor of his cage. "He doesn't recognize the place," I said, trying in vain to make Stanwyck smile. She rang the doorbell a second time. The door opened a crack. Half of Felicity's chalky face was visible. "The macaw? He's all right?" she whispered.

"Oh yes," said Stanwyck. "I'm so grateful to you. The bird helped prove that my father had been hypnotized into a phony confession. Did you know that the bird was the missing link? We want you to come to dinner. You really have saved my father," Stanwyck chatted on. Felicity remained unmoving. She didn't open the door any wider.

"Are you returning the macaw?" she asked, reaching her vein-lined hand through the narrow opening in the door.

"I guess so," said Stanwyck, suddenly quiet. "He's the most beautiful creature. Could I come in to visit the aviary? If not today, another day? Maybe you'd teach me about the

142

birds." Stanwyck spoke eagerly, but the Parrot Woman had no reaction. Her eyes were on the macaw.

We're never going to know how she gets her supply of birds, I thought. If only it didn't matter so much to Stanwyck!

"I'd be careful. I'm very responsible," Stanwyck continued to plead. But the Parrot Woman was impassive.

"It's not possible," Felicity said in her thready voice.

Felicity opened the door and pulled the cage inside. For a moment she touched Stanwyck's hair, and they looked at each other silently. Stanwyck looked up at her, her face full of emotion. She tried to kiss Felicity's cheek, but the woman drew back, startled. "Good-bye," she said crisply, and shut the door. We waited on the step, thinking she might have a change of heart. But a moment later we heard the metallic click of the double locks.

As we crossed Terrapin Circle, I saw the shades in the front room being lowered against the morning light.